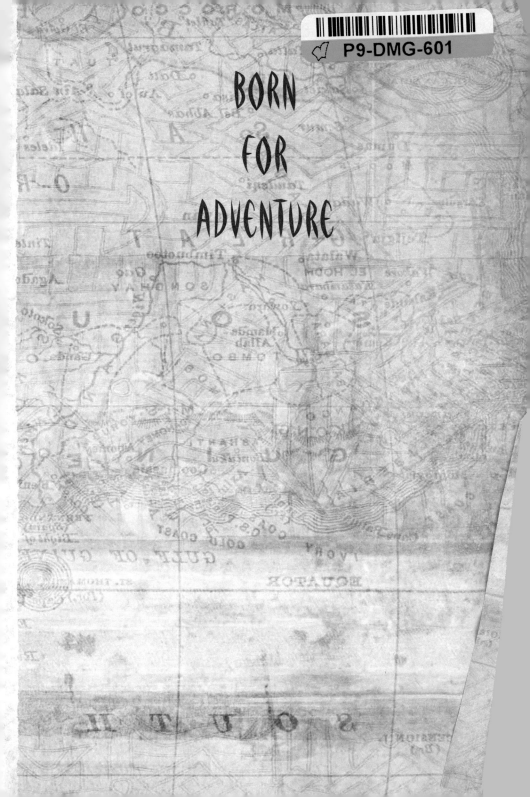

BORN
FOR
ADVENTURE

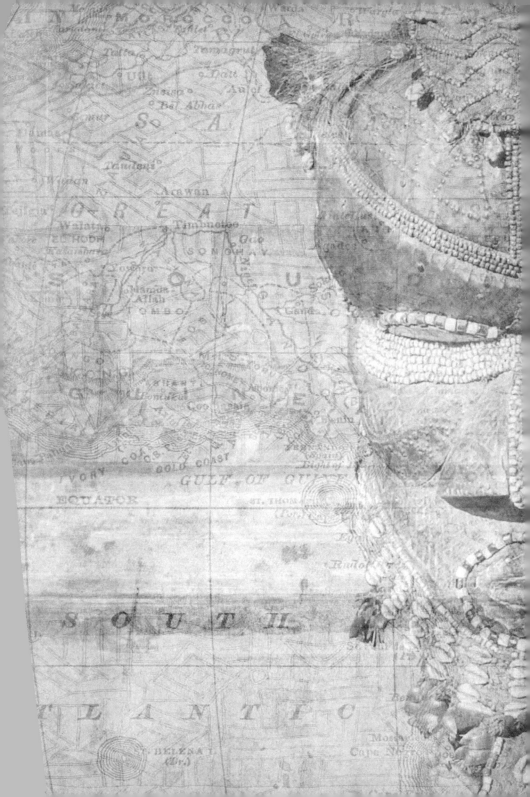

KATHLEEN KARR

BORN FOR ADVENTURE

Marshall Cavendish

Marshall Cavendish Corporation
99 White Plains Road
Tarrytown, NY 10591
www.marshallcavendish.us

Library of Congress Cataloging-in-Publication Data
Karr, Kathleen.
Born for adventure / by Kathleen Karr.
p. cm.
Summary: In 1887, as assistant to Henry Morton Stanley, renowned explorer of the African continent, sixteen-year-old Tom Ormsby makes a perilous trek to help rescue the kidnapped Emin Pasha, learning much about leadership, African people, and himself along the way.
ISBN 978-0-7614-5348-2
[1. Adventure and adventurers—Fiction. 2. Voyages and travels—Fiction. 3. Leadership—Fiction. 4. Emin Pasha Relief Expedition (1887-1889)—Fiction. 5. Stanley, Henry M. (Henry Morton), 1841-1904—Fiction. 6. Africa, Central—History—1884-1960—Fiction.] I. Title.
PZ7.K149Bn 2007
[Fic]—dc22
2006030232

The text of this book is set in Goudy Old Style.
Book design by Anahid Hamparian

Printed in China

First edition
10 9 8 7 6 5 4 3 2 1

mc Marshall Cavendish

For Margery Cuyler—
thanks for being on the same wavelength. . .
most of the time!

In the tropics one must before everything keep calm . . . .
Du calme, du calme.

—Joseph Conrad, *Heart of Darkness*

CONTENTS

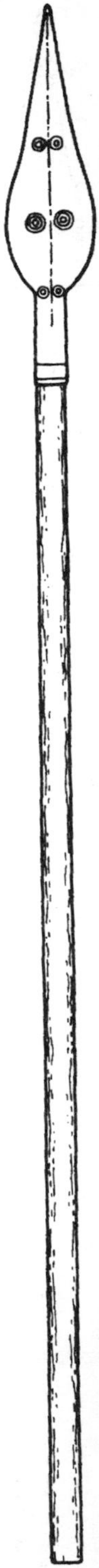

BORN
FOR
ADVENTURE

LONDON

TOM ORMSBY, BORN FOR ADVENTURE.

That's me.

For a cert, the *Adventure* part hadn't presented itself as yet. Else why would I be laboring my way through Burroughs & Wellcome, chemists to the queen? Crawling, in truth. At the ripe old age of sixteen, I hadn't even secured a promotion from a stifling stockroom to an equally claustrophobic clerkship. But like Jack in "Jack Harkaway Among the Sea Fiends of the Moluccas," my favorite boyhood serial, I had pluck.

"Exert yourself, our Tom!" Mum would nag in her daily post-breakfast ritual. With our dad off working the railways, I was the only household male around for her to nag. "Smart as a whip and presentable to boot . . ." at which point she would pause, tsking, and brush down the cowlick that poked up from my sandy hair. Next she'd yank at the front of my green wool jacket—chosen by Herself to "match my eyes." All the while my little sisters would be snickering up their sleeves.

"Instead of moping about with your nose in penny dreadfuls, you could be having the world for your oyster!"

"What's so dreadful about a good cheap read?" I protested this morning as always. "Didn't The Young Englishman teach me ventriloquism and how to copy and write a fine hand? Haven't I progressed to learning geography and the curious habits of far-flung natives from yellowback novels?"

I extracted myself from her attentions to lean against our parlor's mantelpiece in a man-of-the-world pose. Then I went and spoiled the effect by raising my elbow too high, near bringing destruction on the figurines lining the mantel. Steadying the hideous drooling china bulldog in the very nick, I leaped to safer territory before adding my clincher.

"Haven't I studied true Honor and Courage—not to mention Great Britain's Quest for Empire—in real adventures the likes of Henry Morton Stanley's *How I Found Livingstone* and *Through the Dark Continent?*"

Mum gave her apron a derisive tug. "Stanley's an *American*."

"A *Welshman* first," I insisted.

"That's not the kind of exertion I'll be thinking on! More like a steady and reliable show at work. It pays to be steady and reliable, our Tom. Folks take notice!"

Too right. And keep a fellow at his steady and reliable job till doomsday. *Blast.* Everything always came back to my bloody apprenticeship, didn't it? The Ormsby family's hopes of rising from the working to the middle class lay squarely on my shoulders. And with my training completed, what lay before me? The prospect of another fifty years imprisoned by shelves filled with dusty bottles of quinine. Quinine for the fever lands of the Empire: India . . . the Far East . . . *Africa.*

"Here now, Mum." I bent to enfold her comfortably plump little body in a hug. It was always a wonder to me why my literary heroes never considered the option of giving hugs first, instead of embarking straightaway on violent action. A well-timed hug covered a multitude of sins. I winked at Katie and Hannah, then threw my ventriloquist voice to the mantel, setting the bulldog into a fierce growl. Over their delighted shrieks, I took my leave.

"Top-notch breakfast, but I must be off to work."

I muffled myself against London's biting January and headed for Burroughs & Wellcome—with only a short detour to the closest news agent.

Arriving at work, I studied the bold headlines blaring from the newspaper I'd picked up. It was the talk of all the papers, all of London, all of England:

EMIN PASHA BESIEGED!
ANOTHER KHARTOUM?

The very word *Khartoum* was enough to chill me worse than the weather. Only two years past this very January, General Charles George Gordon was utterly destroyed in his Soudanese desert fortress on the Nile by the so-called Mahdi, or New Prophet, and his dervish armies—in the name of Allah and Islam. And not only "Chinese Gordon," but his entire British garrison. Over ten thousand people! England had sent help too late to end the ten-month siege. After our soldiers had surrendered and been disarmed, the merciless Mahdists slaughtered every last one of them, from Gordon on down. The garrison's innocent children were dragged off into slavery. Even worse, the garrison's innocent women were dragged off into *harems*.

And now the same mad Mahdist armies had marched south from the Soudan and were besieging this Emin Pasha fellow—like Gordon, the legitimate representative of our Empire—in Equatoria. Was the British Lion to cower before them yet again?

"No!" I smashed my fist into the newspaper. "Our colonies are as sacred as our English soil!"

"What are you nattering on about, Tom? You'd best get on with packing before old Crockett steps back with his cup of tea. Can't keep the great Stanley waiting, can we?"

I glowered at Jones-Smythe, fellow sufferer in the stockroom, then thought better of it. The poor chap was having a particularly pink and pimply day. Shoving aside the paper, I consulted my master list. Checked the careful ticks. One indispensable item was still lacking. I gave the wheeled ladder a shove down the stockroom aisle, then clambered up it, passing shelf after shelf after overflowing shelf of every powdered, liquid, and tablet medication known to modern man. In the rarefied heights just below the tin ceiling, I spied my quarry.

"Hah. Just the ticket to soothe the savage bowel!" After blowing years of accumulated dust off the bottles, I stuffed my pockets with Dr. J. Collis Browne's Chlorodyne—known to the world at large as Dr. Collis Brown's—then made my descent with the aplomb of a seasoned mountaineer.

On terra firma again, I polished the bottles to a high gloss and bent to tuck them into the last empty slots of the waiting case. "Done." I gave the other contents a final flick of my rag. "Well done indeed."

A snicker from beyond. "Taking more of a proprietary interest than usual, ain't you, Tom?"

I ignored Jones-Smythe, he of the stunted imagination. Before me sat one of the medical kits my firm was donating to the great explorer Henry Morton Stanley's latest expedition of mercy into the darkest part of the Darkest Continent: *the Congo and Equatoria*. Stanley would find the beleaguered Emin Pasha. Not that I gave a fig who Emin Pasha was—nor did the rest of Britain, either. Was the principle of the thing, wasn't it? But Stanley'd find the man in time, saving him from the fanatic dervish legions waging a holy war against British rule in the name of Islam. Stanley would keep the British Union Jack flying over our farthest outpost.

And here was I, Tom Ormsby, contributing to the rescue effort. Would that I could do more.

I ran a hand lovingly over the chest's polished wood. It was stocked with every medication known to combat the diseases peculiar to Africa—but most especially quinine, endless amounts of quinine, to counter the equatorial fevers. Lush forests and raging rivers swam before my eyes. Enough of "steady and reliable!" Ah, to take off for the unknown, to set my strength against such obstacles. What were a few blood-sucking insects or ravaging tribes against the Course of Empire?

"Ormsby!"

My head shot up from the neat compartments. Crockett had returned. "Sir?"

"Mr. Wellcome requires a lad to see the first shipment to Stanley's quarters—"

"Sir!"

I rolled down my sleeves, flew into my coat, and set off from the Snowhill buildings on the mission that would change my life.

Vans delivering every imaginable commodity piled up before the great Stanley's home in a bedlam of steaming, snorting horses and rising voices. Directing my drayman to take his place among them, I ignored the polished brass sign affixed on the wrought iron fence next to the gate:

TRADESMEN'S ENTRANCE

TO THE REAR

Instead I headed importantly to the front door with Burroughs & Wellcome's bill of lading in hand. Yanked the bell pull. In short order a butler was inspecting me.

"Your purpose?"

"Mr. Stanley's personal signature is required—"

He wearily waved me past the mountains of boxes and crates cluttering the entryway and grand room beyond. "You may join the end of the queue forming on the staircase."

The line was long and moved slowly. I shuffled upward, eavesdropping on the conversation between two stiff-necked army officers ahead of me.

"Barttelot, Edmund Musgrave. Major. Seventh Fusiliers."

A curt nod of acknowledgment. "Nelson, R. H. Captain. Methuen's Horse."

"I say,"—Barttelot slapped his swagger stick on his palm— "aren't you the chap who distinguished himself in the Zulu campaigns?"

The captain puffed his chest fair gaudy with medals. "Saw a bit of action."

"So you're for the expedition, too."

"Won't leave the old man's office till he offers me articles of agreement."

A shiver ran through my spine as I moved another two steps up. I was standing in an employment line for Stanley's Relief of Emin Pasha Expedition! Does opportunity knock twice? Without a second thought, I shoved the bill of lading into my pocket, straightened my collar, and tightened the knot of my black cravat. Assumed the ramrod military stance of the gentlemen before me and considered what my hero Jack Harkaway would do in this selfsame situation.

Applicants pressed forward. . . . Applicants disappeared into Stanley's office.

Suddenly it was my turn. And there he was in the flesh: *Henry Morton Stanley*. He sat behind a paper-littered desk, gray head bowed over his pen. Much older than I'd imagined.

"Name!" he barked.

I steeled myself "Thomas . . ." Why not award myself a middle name as good as those officers on the staircase? As good as Stanley's? "Thomas *Grenville* Ormsby. Sir."

The great Stanley's head popped up. Shrewd gray eyes examined me as he stroked a drooping end of his mustache.

"Position requested?"

"General dogsbody, sir."

"What can you do that my African boy, Baruti, can't?"

"I've some chemist training, and I'm a whip hand with inventories. . . ."

"Quartermastering, eh?"

"Yes, sir." I remembered reading about the pilferage problems he'd had on his earlier expeditions. "Some things are best left in guaranteed honest hands, sir."

Those eyes set into a hard squint. "Age?"

"Eighteen." I secretly crossed my fingers. In about a year and a half, God willing.

A yank at his mustache. "A bit young, wouldn't you say?"

"I believe you served in the American Civil War at a similar age. Sir."

He smiled. "Touché. I like your attitude, young Ormsby. Health?"

I pounded my chest. "Robust."

"Good. That will help with the statistics."

"Statistics, sir?"

He raised an eyebrow. "One in three white men going into Dark Africa is dead within the year."

I tried for a nonchalant shrug. "Oh, *those* statistics."

A half smile this time. "A man willing to take on the odds. Even better. Your references?"

"First thing in the morning, sir."

"Excellent. You may sign your papers then."

Papers. The bill of lading burned a hole in my pocket. In for a penny . . . I pulled it out and presented it with a bow. "If I might have your signature first, sir?"

The mighty explorer frowned over the neat tally, quickly put two and two together—and *chuckled.* "You have got pluck, Ormsby." He signed with a flourish. "The most valuable commodity of all in the bush." Then Stanley thrust out his hand for mine. Shook. "The expedition sails on the twentieth of January. Next!"

I marched from his office and reeled down the stairs.

Sail on January 20? Less than a fortnight from today? To Africa? With the great Henry Morton Stanley? . . . And references? No one ever askped penny dreadful heroes for references!

7

My steady and reliable world shattered around me. What had I done?

"**Africa!**" Mum screeched as I announced the news that evening.

"You did say to exert myself," I pointed out, not unreasonably, I thought.

"But Africa!" She clutched at her bosom, gasping for breath.

"Deepest Darkest Africa," I added with satisfaction. "The Congo."

Next came the tears, worthy of an equatorial monsoon. Katie ran to put the teakettle on the hob. Eyes wide, Hannah sat coiled on the overstuffed sofa. She plunged a thumb into her mouth, then extracted it to ask, "Will you bring me a black baby, our Tom? Like we gives pennies for at church?"

Sigh. "I can't be taking a baby from its own mum, Hannah, but I'll bring you something." I wrapped my arms around my rapidly disintegrating mother. "It's not forever, Mum. And I'll be signing half my pay over to you—"

A great convulsive sob. "*How* long?"

Luckily I'd pulled myself together from the morning interview in time to have a little chat with Henry Stanley's all-knowing butler. "Mr. Stanley, he figures two months by ship to Matadi. That's the town nearest the mouth of the Congo. Then a short walk up to Stanley Pool—named after his own self! Can you only picture a place named after me?" I rushed on. "Next a pleasant steamboat cruise farther up the river and a more or less straight trek through the bush to where this Emin Pasha fellow has got himself in hot water . . ."

Mum had stopped listening. And sobbing, too. She groped for a vast handkerchief and blew. A hiccup of recovery, followed by, "Lake Ormsby? Wouldn't that be the very thing to make the neighbors take notice!"

"Well, it could be a river," I allowed. "Or even a mountain . . ."

"Still and all," Mum said. "And you'll be back in just a few months?"

"Well . . . eight or ten. A year at the top."

"Sooner than one of them London Missionary Society folks the pastor is always begging us to support!"

Perfect introduction to what I had to ask next. "Which reminds me, Mum. Would you go with me to see Pastor Gribbins? I'll need a letter of reference from him for Mr. Stanley in the morning—"

Mum shook herself back into her usual indomitable self. "I'll stand over the old sourpuss till he does you justice. You can be sure of that! Only think on the good you can be doing amongst them poor heathens. Katie! Where's that tea? A good stiff cup, and I can be taking on every last hellfire and brimstone Nonconformist Methodist your benighted dad's thrust on me. Why I had to fall for a bloke outside the Church of England—"

Katie shoved a steaming cup into Mum's hands, ending the familiar diatribe. A therapeutic swallow, then, "Best be taking the stew off the fire, daughter. Next bundle up your sister and yourself. We're stepping out for a visit!"

So it was that I received the first of two excellent references to present to Henry Morton Stanley before noon the next day.

Pastor Gribbins's long dour face had actually creaked— painfully—into a thin-lipped smile.

"Black souls, Thomas. Heaven is hungry for black souls!" He presented me with a new Bible. "To think *you* would be chosen to carry the Word!"

"But I'm only a dogsbody. . . ."

"Such modesty is becoming." He carefully smoothed stray hairs across his bald pate. Sober black they were, like his suit. "Remember well: ordination is not a prerequisite for the job, young man. Christian witness has been known to work miracles."

When he was done praying over me, I rushed for the welcome cold of the winter night. Sucked up its chill till Mum and the girls caught up and I was calmer. Suddenly everyone wanted to own a piece of me and Africa. . . . Hopefully my

9

employers' demands would be more reasonable.

When I approached them first thing the next morning, Messrs. Burroughs and Wellcome were so honored by the expedition's acceptance of one of their own employees, that their letter of recommendation had only the faintest toehold on reality. Their lone stricture was to "keep a sharp eye out for the effectiveness" of their nostrums. "Have to keep abreast of science and the competition, eh, lad? Er, young man." A pat on the back from Burroughs.

From Wellcome, "Your glorious return will surely see a marked change in your position within our estimable firm, Ormsby."

I near gagged at the thought of a return to all I was escaping but managed to bob my head with sufficient enthusiasm. "Indeed, a prospect I shall look forward to, sir."

So it was that I sailed away from all I had ever known.

Right on schedule I embarked on the SS *Navarino* the afternoon of January 20, 1887, the Golden Jubilee Year of our own Victoria, Queen of Great Britain and Ireland and Empress of India. I stood as tall as a giant among the officers and goods of the Expedition for the Relief of Emin Pasha, drinking in the crowd of well-wishers gathered for our send-off. The God speeds from the dock were heartiest from the staff of Burroughs & Wellcome. The entire office had been given a half holiday in honor of my leave-taking, after all. I feared for the pubs that shortly would receive their custom. But it was the tiny cluster at the very tip of the quay that held my eyes . . . and my heart. Katie and Hannah bounced with excitement, their flaxen braids streaming behind them as they waved their little Union Jacks. My mother gripped her new lace bonnet against the freshening wind with one hand, while swabbing her glistening face with the other.

"Never fear, Mum!" I shouted hoarsely over the growing rumble of the steamer's engines as the distance from the dock widened. "I'll be writing regular!"

I loosed whitened knuckles from the railing to grapple for one of the huge handkerchiefs Mum had stocked in all my pockets. Jack Harkaway never bowed to sentiment. But I was Tom Ormsby.

I blew my nose lustily.

THE VOYAGE

FROM THE MOMENT MY ARTICLES WERE SIGNED IN the distant winter of London, I'd had high hopes that my voyage would be accomplished within the good fellowship of a glorious band of comrades.

Bleeding wrong.

Captain R. H. Nelson of Methuen's Horse was indeed among the chosen. As was Major Edmund Musgrave Barttelot of the 7th Fusiliers, a Lieutenant W. Grant Stairs of the Royal Engineers, a Mr. A. J. Monteney Jephson, and a few others who'd join us later in the voyage. The quay barely out of sight, I approached Nelson with the swagger of the elect.

"Begging your pardon, Captain?" I paused while he noted my presence. Introduced myself by name—complete with the "Grenville"—as Stanley's special assistant. Then, "What is the drill to be, sir? For the length of the voyage? Dining and such, since we're members of the same expedition—"

"The drill?" He snickered. "Barttelot. This fellow wants to know about the shipboard *drill!*"

Major Barttelot strode closer and glanced down his nose at me. His mustache quivered. "Stanley's personal servant? Never have shared a mess with servants. Never intend to start."

Off they sauntered, chuckling while they pulled out cigars for a convivial smoke.

Cut cold.

I gripped the railing in anger. I was considered to be Stanley's servant, was I? And me trained in *trade*, not *service*. I glowered at the insult, till common sense took over. The distinction was like to make me as arrogant as those officers. I'd signed on to do anything, hadn't I? By Heaven, if Stanley needed a servant, I'd learn how to be the best there was! Still and all . . .

I raised my eyes to the fast disappearing port, to the tugs and barges and coasters that crowded the busy Thames channel around us. Wasn't "serving" the job of Stanley's black boy, Baruti? Baruti, who'd gotten himself lost somewhere in the city of London and missed the boat. A Mr. William Bonny had been dispatched to find the African and catch up with the expedition on another ship. Now I hadn't even Baruti for the learning. Would it have been a different story if the great Stanley had joined us on the *Navarino*? But our leader was completing business in London, then Cairo. I'd see none of him till we reached the Suez. The truth dawned on me at last. I was on my own.

Bloody Hell.

I stayed on deck till an evening fog enveloped the Thames as it widened into its estuary. Listening to the engines throb as the ship made for the North Sea; watching the lights of other vessels blink and dim in the swirling mists as they slid past us; shivering within my muffler and greatcoat from insult, injury, and cold. Only when the sharp, clean winds leached the anger from me did I finally go in search of my supper and my quarters.

We hugged the coasts of France and Spain those first few fog-bound, stormy days. I saw none of them. I had my eyes squinched shut in prayer so fervent even Pastor Gribbins would've been impressed. Mind you, that's when I wasn't bemoaning every bite I'd swallowed during the only meal I'd managed to take at my assigned second sitting in the dining saloon—or endlessly upchucking that selfsame meal. Followed by what felt like all my innards.

Curses on being lowest in the pecking order. Curses on the whole bloody pecking system!

My groans filled the cubbyhole well below decks that was my lot. Right next to the engines, it was. Pounding engines. Stomach-churning, incredibly stinking engines. And nary a porthole to freshen the air. Hellish heat combined with the stench of machinery and slops, with the rolling and the tossing . . . the tossing and the rolling. . . .

Misery. Hour upon hour of it . . . Was Africa worth it? . . . Would I live to see Africa? . . . Would they send my body back to Mum or just toss me overboard, into the merciless waves?

Bam!

Someone, something at the door. "Go away," I begged.

Bam! Bam!

"Just let me die!"

The door swung wide.

"Eh, laddie—" Huge hands yanked me from my bunk and hauled me from my torture chamber. "Enough o' stinkin' up the whole bloody engine room. Enough o' the moans an' groans like some doom-bearin' banshee. Hell's bones! Settin' me men on edge, it is. Past time ye found yere sea legs."

"What legs?" I whimpered. The quaking mass of jelly I was swaying upon?

He tossed me toward some stairs. "Climb!"

With that great brute at my back, I crawled up a flight . . . then another . . . and yet more—to sprawl at last flat on my face above decks. In the frigid air.

"Breathe!" the monster ordered.

I gasped for the coldness. Swallowed some . . . more—

"That'll do. Haul yereself up."

Jack Harkaway never had to put up with such a beast. But then, Jack Harkaway never got seasick. "Can't!" I groaned.

"This be the kind o' help the great Stanley hires for his expedition? Be ye a man or a quiverin', cowerin' mousie?"

He spat past my head in disgust. I managed to raise myself enough to watch the blob swallowed by an incoming wave that sloshed over the railing and doused me, through and through. The icy water finally cleared my head. The insult registered.

"Here now!" I stumbled to my feet and shakily cocked my fists. "No one mocks Mr. Stanley in my hearing!"

"Aye, that'll be more like it." He captured a fist with an oil-stained mitt and shook. "Alexander McNabb, chief engineer."

Another wave knocked me near into his arms. "Tom Ormsby." I staggered, managing a grin. "Born for Adventure."

His tremendous hoot floored me again. "There's a few lessons ye'll be needin' if ye're to be survivin' *Adventure*, laddie. But first things first." He yanked me, flopping like a fish, from the sloshing deck. "An' that'll be a wee dram to settle the stomach."

Alexander McNabb was my saving. Who'd want to waste precious time with Barttelot & Company when there were the mysteries of engines to explore? Short an engine mate, the chief put me to work straightaway. Soon I was spending my days stripped to the waist, black as any African. A wrench in one hand, I'd lean over McNabb as he lubricated a piston rod or crankshaft.

"Mind the flywheel, Tom. And steer clear of the exhaust—"

Whooooosh.

"Losh, man! Dinna I just now say to mind the exhaust?"

"Sorry, chief."

"It's sorry ye'll be if I don't be gettin' some engine grease on that steam burn, and soon." He hauled me off to slather thick goo across my chest, just the way Mum cured all burns with her butter.

Only Mum wouldn't be muttering oaths the entire time. He finished with, "An' if it wasn't me down one man, ye think I'd be takin' the trouble?"

I grinned through the steam and headed back to the bank of engines. I was fascinated by how they were all put together, how they generated power. And when our watch was over, we'd go above decks where the chief gave me some proper boxing lessons.

"Hands up! Protect yereself, laddie! Now duck—"

"*Oow!*" Wasn't any joke coming up against the chief's mighty right hook.

"Duck faster, like it was the poison arrows o' them Congo cannibals comin' at ye!"

Poison arrows? Nobody'd said anything about poison arrows. As for cannibals—

"*Oof.*"

"Off the deck." Alexander McNabb hulked over me, clucking in disgust. "Think, man. Build eyes all about yere head. Figure where the punch's comin' from afore it hits ye."

Gritting my teeth, I dragged myself up for another round. Learned to step faster and duck lower. Along the way I must have passed some kind of test, because just under the huge purple shadow of the Rock of Gibraltar, McNabb led me to his sea chest. Lovingly extracting a long, wrapped object, he handed it to me.

"What is it?"

"A rifle. A Martini Henry rifle. The verra gun as keeps order through our whole blessed Empire. Single shot. Fast. Reliable as me engines." He reached back into his chest for an ammunition case. "Never been up the Congo proper, but I hear tell it has ferocious beasties—crocs, an' hippos, and the Almighty only knows what else. Betimes ye find yereself wi' trouble, won't be amiss to know the shootin'."

I unwrapped the weapon and admired it, from the polished wooden stock to the long barrel he'd greased as well as his engines. I peered through its sights. "What do we shoot at?"

"Them flocks o' useless gulls that's been followin' us, for starters."

I lowered the barrel. "They remind me of home."

McNabb snorted. "Aye, be that chicken-hearted when ye come against true danger, ye'll never make it up the Congo."

With true regret, I lay down the weapon. "Sorry, chief, but if they're not trying to eat me, and I'm not hungry enough to eat them—"

"Losh, man." He heaved a great sigh and rubbed at the orange stubble bristling his cheeks. "A'weel . . . Seems like we'll be startin' wi' empty tins, then."

Bobbing on lengths of rope in the smooth waters of the Mediterranean, the tins were large enough targets to give a sweaty-palmed beginner like me hope for some measure of success. Once I stopped toppling backward from the recoil and steadied my hands enough to actually aim, Chief Engineer McNabb lengthened the lines, adding more of a challenge to the endeavor.

The marksmanship lessons would've been a fair lark if our daily practice hadn't dredged up Barttelot & Company. At first the officers merely lounged about, trying to top each others' snide remarks. But the more their insults rankled, the more I improved . . . till they hauled out their own rifles.

No surprise, they went straight for the gulls. I bit my tongue and increased my concentration on the bobbing tins. Yet, from the corner of my eye, I couldn't help but see Major Barttelot bring down first one, then another of the carefree swooping birds. Right. Point proven. The man could shoot. When he raised his rifle a third time, my gorge rose—along with an irresistible impulse. How long since I'd practiced my ventriloquism skills? Were they lost? Maybe not . . .

"*What the deuce—*"

The cigar gripped between the major's teeth fell to the deck as he stared slack-jawed at his rifle barrel. And why shouldn't he be staring? It was humming "Rule Britannia." On key, too.

I made it through an entire verse and chorus before Alexander McNabb gave me a subtle—for him—elbow jab. His knowing grin was fierce, but his message clear. "Ye'd best be takin' another pot-shot at them tins, laddie. Before the jig is up."

I aimed with abandon. "Bull's-eye!" Reloaded in record time. "Another!"

My reward was a backslap that near sent me and the chief's precious Martini Henry rifle into the sea.

"Ye're improvin' apace, Tom. Keep it up, an' them Congo crocs won't stand a chance."

On the 6th of February my idyll ended. The *Navarino* steamed into Suez Harbor, cut engines, and dropped anchor. Shortly thereafter, Mr. Stanley boarded.

"I say, engine boy?" Major Barttelot's voice lazily drifted down the companionway. "Mr. Stanley is asking for his *servant*."

The chief handed me a greasy rag. "The Day o' Reckonin'." He sighed. "Had to come. 'Tis a pity. With another month or two under my wing, you could o' been sittin' for your mate's ticket."

Henry Morton Stanley's arrival sped from my mind. "I've learned nearly enough to be licensed? Truly?"

"Aye. Truly. Ye've got the aptitude for the work. Beyond a doot. A fine ear for the gears what might be overstrained. A ready boot for the stubborn wheel . . ."

Conflict beset me. Would not a career under the wing of Chief Engineer Alexander McNabb be glorious? Friendly and comfortable, too. He caught the look on my face and interpreted it correctly. There never was a man for reading me the way he could. Running an oily hand through his wild mop of hair, he sighed again.

"Be off with ye, laddie. Ye've given yere word. A true man stands by his honor an' his word."

Honor. It was beginning to take on new meanings.

"Aye aye, sir." I gave him my first and last salute. Then I reached for my shirt and marched toward the ladder and my new master.

TO ZANZIBAR AND BEYOND

IT WAS BARUTI I SAW FIRST. HE WAS HARD TO MISS, dressed to the nines as he was in his London finery despite the heat. He wasn't a *boy*, either. More near a man than me.

A real African from the Congo.

I fear I stared as he towered behind Stanley, mahogany handsome. Absolutely *towered*. I dropped my eyes at last. Away from his desk, the mighty Henry Morton Stanley was a very short man— truly, not much above Mum's height! I wiped the shock from my face as he paced the deck in his crisp tropical whites, cockily tossing out orders.

"Ormsby!" He finally noticed me.

"Sir!" I snapped to attention.

He nodded toward the harbor. I squinted through the midday haze to focus on a barge lumbering toward us behind a puffing steam launch. It seemed to be filled with—

"See the livestock is properly stowed and tended. Should we decide to take the overland route to Emin Pasha from Zanzibar, it will prove invaluable." He flicked the dog whip in his hand for emphasis, then was apparently done with me. "Shall we assay our quarters, Baruti?"

Stanley spun and headed below deck, Baruti following like a faithful hound. That left me with the care and feeding of forty *donkeys*. No point in even trying to figure what rung that was in the bloody system. Behind me, I heard Barttelot snicker.

The Suez Canal had no locks, and the Red Sea was black. The Arabian Peninsula was naught but barren sandy desert with a scattering of camels. There was sufficient time for me to make these observations, since I spent the following days and nights en route to Aden above deck, keeping an eye on my donkeys. I'd corralled them in the only available space—the ship's stern, just aft of the ventilators and downwind of the funnels, where blasts of sooty exhaust soon turned their soft brown hides to black. I tried currying the coal soot off them, but had long since given up on getting my own hide clean. Not that I really minded either the dirt or the livestock. Truth be told, these asses were gentle, affectionate creatures, and not much smellier than the chief's engine room—only a different kind of smelly . . . richly animal.

Two Egyptian boys robed in flowing *gallibyas*, heads wrapped in white turbans—sensible, cool clothing I soon envied—had come with them as keepers. Abdullah and Hamid and I struck up a comfortable working relationship. In the course of this, I learned a few things about donkeys and more than a few exotic oaths. Of Baruti I saw nothing but his black shadow ever present behind Stanley during their daily constitutionals.

I never did get ashore in Aden, though by this time I fair hungered for land—hungered to the point of near leaping next to the mailbag in the bobbing launch that carried my letters for home. As the small boat readied itself to ferry mail and expedition officers to the nearest dock, I consoled myself with the fact that the colony was nothing more than a seafront of muddy buildings hunkered down beneath jagged chocolate-colored mountains. Didn't help, did it? Also didn't help when Barttelot hesitated on the gangway ladder and glanced at me moping over the railing. "Oh, donkey captain?" he called, then topped his insult with a snide salute.

"Better to be the head of an ass than the tail of a horse!" I shot back.

Fortunately he'd clambered out of hearing, so I shrugged it all off and began overseeing the transfer of my long-eared charges to our next steamer, via the barge that was snugging up to our hull. Wasn't an easy task. The donkeys' own land hunger, as they smelled it so temptingly close, set them into brays and stomps. But by dint of the carrot and the stick, the job was accomplished—me concentrating on the carrot part, leaving the sticks for Abdullah and Hamid.

The fact is, my "carrot" was *bread*. Early on, I'd discovered that the beasts ignored the hay I'd lay out next to their water troughs in favor of sly attacks on my picnic bread rations. So when it came time to strap the animals in slings to be lowered to the waiting barge, I calmed them with chunks of white bread begged from the galley.

As for Abdullah and Hamid's sticks . . . one was a good stout cudgel vigorously applied to the balking donkeys' rear quarters. The other was a goad—a wand that had a bit of a pin sticking out. A prick or two to the rump got the beasts moving in my direction right sharpish. Could've done with a little less cudgeling enthusiasm, though. Could've done without the boys' jeers, too. My donkeys weren't "stupid louts." They had a good sense of self-preservation is all. When I voiced both thoughts, the Egyptians' reply was, "*Donkey* Tom!"

Besides leaving me exhausted and sweat stained, the exercise also left me wondering how any beast of burden survived in lands with such a cudgel-and-prod philosophy of animal husbandry.

Then there was me, stranded aboard the *Oriental*, with the *Navarino*—gently swaying so teasingly close to us in Aden's harbor—due to proceed east to Bombay. As we weighed anchor for Mombasa and points south, I spied Alexander McNabb's great hulk leaning over the *Navarino's* starboard side, puffing at his pipe. I waved both arms like a semaphore, desperately wanting to broach the distance. He raised a fist in answer—and the *Oriental's* horn blasted through the stifling afternoon. All forty donkeys kicked and brayed in a frenzy of terror.

"Here now." I abandoned McNabb and the railing to bend over the closest donkey. Gave it a hug.

If Mum could see me now.

I finally got shore leave on the island of Zanzibar, lying just off east Africa and south of the equator—all on account of my blessed donkeys. For it was in Zanzibar that Stanley stopped toying with the idea of taking the short route across the island's channel to the continent itself, and the Emin Pasha's relief, because the inland natives were on the warpath. Since donkeys couldn't be easily used in the Congo, they were to be sold off here. In the midst of the busy harbor filled with German battleships, merchant vessels, and scores of darting dhows, I vigorously oversaw their offloading and bade farewell to Abdullah and Hamid.

Hallelujah. A taste of freedom at last!

Under an impossibly blue tropical sky I set off past the wharves to test my land legs. Finally, I could see firsthand a genuine exotic port, the stuff I'd been daydreaming about for years. I'd only swayed a dozen yards

"*Baksheesh! Baksheesh!*"

"Blazes!" A mob of beggar boys! Slapping them off did as little good as trying to attack a swarm of mosquitoes. And I didn't fancy squandering my first expedition wages on them. Fair desperate, I yelled, "Anybody speak English?"

A miniature tatter-robed African fought his way front and center. "Me, boss. Seyyid. Speak good."

His tight wiry hair haloed around his grubby turban, making his dark face and skinny neck stand out like an artichoke on its stem. Ribs poked from his half-bared chest. Looked like he could do with a decent meal.

"Right. Get rid of the rest of the fellows and you can be my guide."

Seyyid smiled like the sun dawning over the sea, then turned into a dynamo worthy of McNabb's engine room. I watched, awestruck. Kicks, punches, bites, curses . . . and lo, the field was clear. I was now the proud employer of my very own guide to Zanzibar. He took his job seriously, too. A satisfied shake of his robes and he commenced.

"There, boss," he pointed. "Ivory."

"Ivory?" The skirmish had distracted me from the obvious. Walling the road to town were crisscrossed stacks of huge crescent shapes, rising higher than the roof of our brick two-story house back in London.

"Tooth of elephant." He mimicked long tusks growing from his chin. "Polish shiny, good for things. One elephant own two tusks. Take one elephant, make one piano."

I stopped cold before the sight, trying to work my gaping jaw shut. Mum and the girls had been campaigning for a piano ever since I could remember. "Such a *civilized* instrument," Mum always said to our dad. "Set the girls up in society proper, a piano would."

Bleeding misery.

Here was I looking at thousands of tusks, waiting to be loaded and shipped to Europe, to England. For piano keys. I glared down at my guide. "What happens to the rest of the elephant?"

He shrugged. Slid a finger across his throat.

My legs stayed frozen. I'd seen an elephant once at the London Zoo. Alive. "But they're great bloody beasts. . . ."

Seyyid nodded with enthusiasm. "Beautiful teeth worth eight shillings a pound!" He tugged at my arm, and we began moving past the chalky white mortuary. "Zanzibar live on ivory, live on slaves—"

I stopped short again. "But slavery's been banned."

"Allah be praised, not in Zanzibar!"

Zanzibar Town was an eye-opener. It had a top-notch, modern clock tower and had coconut palms lining a grand avenue leading to a spanking new sultan's palace. It had horses and carriages and lamp posts as good as London. It had officers and sailors from the seven seas riding in the carriages and promenading the avenue, mixing with Africans and Abyssinians and fiercely haughty, fork-bearded Arabs with lethal scimitars shoved through the belts of their robes. Those scimitars caught my fancy for a cert. *Bloody marvelous.* What couldn't I do with one of those fine curved blades! Be the envy of Jones-Smythe and every other fellow back at Burroughs & Wellcome, I would. But I wasn't setting foot back in Burroughs & Wellcome. Ever. Still and all . . .

Zanzibar also had ladies completely covered from head to toe. Wrapped tight as Christmas packages, they were. I couldn't stop staring. Seyyid tugged at me.

"Not to look at womens, boss. Big trouble."

"But how can they see to cart their water jugs? How can they keep a lookout for all those children tagging behind them?"

He cupped his hands and raised them to his eyes like binoculars. "Small, very small opening. With veil. My mother see."

"Doesn't she complain?" An unknown word. "Doesn't it make her *unhappy?*"

"Not no more. Not since fever took her."

"Oh." Stumped for proper words of sympathy, I glanced around, seeking to divert both of us. We'd wandered away from the fancy avenue into a teeming bazaar, part sprawling under the sky, part winding into narrow streets beyond.

Bleeding wonder. This was a bit more like it!

The open square was tightly filled with canopied stalls of cloth and rugs and metalwork and spices and strange accumulations of—

"What in Heaven's name?" I gawked at a booth festooned

with clusters of dried lizards and frogs, jars heaped with insect parts and tiny bones, vials filled with gooey bloodlike syrups, and more . . . indescribably more.

"Charm things, boss. For talismans." Seyyid yanked at a small cloth bag that hung from his neck. "Keep away bad spirits. Make luck. You want? Medicine lady fix for you!"

The medicine lady in question hove into view. She was gargantuan. Miles of cloth enwrapped her, wicked claw marks defaced her cheeks, and braids swirled 'round her head like some black Medusa. She leaned toward me, pointing a finger.

"Gulai sees you, bwana," she intoned. "Gulai sees dark days coming. Gulai fix."

"No . . . no thank you all the same, ma'am."

Shivering, I bolted from her cavernous eyes. I fled toward the nearest archway, those eyes following, then flew deeper and deeper into the labyrinthine passageways of the endless bazaar. Seyyid scrambled after me. Wasn't till I broke into the light of day again—to steam rising from bubbling cauldrons—that I slowed down at last. I exorcised the witch from my mind with one sniff. Interesting smells . . . exotic smells . . . came at me from those cauldrons, from scores of smoky grills. Could feel my empty stomach stand up and salute.

"Would you care to join me for some dinner, Seyyid?"

He was doubled over, his chest heaving. "*Now*, boss?" A pained gasp. "After so much running?"

"Yes—no!" Another stall caught my attention. It was a stall exhibiting knives sharp enough to cut through the haze surrounding us . . . scimitars. Their allure overwhelmed me. "Let's just have a look at these first."

I pounced on the display. So taken was I by a particularly fine specimen in a brass-studded sheath, that I near laid down the entire contents of my pockets for its possession.

"Wait!" Seyyid yelped, having recovered in the nick of time. He snatched my coins of the realm from the counter and shoved them back at me. Then he turned on the merchant, putting an end to the man's gleeful hand rubbing. "What kind of price you give my friend for bad blade?" Yanking the knife from its fancy sheath, Seyyid sliced at his robe, without effect. "What kind of steel? Pah!" He flung it down.

"A moment! A moment!" The Arab rushed for another scimitar hidden behind him, slid it from its sheath, and sliced his own robe. "The best! Like razor. I swear by the Prophet! Give good price."

Seyyid sneered at the price. Quartered it. Much venting of spleen followed as both reverted to what had to be Swahili—since it didn't sound much like Abdullah and Hamid's Arabic—before apparently coming to a mutual conclusion. Seyyid poked me.

"Is good price now, boss."

I frowned. "But that's one-third of his first price!"

"Right price. Always one-third of first price. Pay."

I bought my very own scimitar. Enchanted by these novel techniques of bargaining, I dragged Seyyid past the food stalls to test my own skills in the purchase of souvenirs for the family. Handwoven cloth in bold African colors was just the trick for Mum. A wide hammered-copper plate for our dad's Sunday roast beef. Exotic black dolls with braidable hair for the girls. That accomplished, my guide looked near faint from the aromas floating through the air. I gave him his head at last.

"Time for our stomachs now. You navigate."

Seyyid did. Round the pots of goat stew and odd-looking fish and—

"Hell's bones! What's *that?*" Something beyond strange on a grill . . .

"Ho, boss."

Seyyid's eyes blazed with desire. Could almost see him salivating.

"Very special. Very, very special. Dhows bring from far, far. Is Giant Madagascar Hissing Cockroach!"

My stomach lurched as I chanced a second look. Eight-inch, ten-inch *bugs*. Merrily waving their antennae and hissing as they sizzled. I gagged and propelled Seyyid away from temptation.

"No, boss?" His lament was pitiful.

"No. Absolutely not. In fact, *never*."

I settled on the goat stew. I could live with what it came from. Then we squatted in the dust, plunging our hands into a common bowl while the heat hung full over everything . . . pressing down on the bazaar . . . pressing down on Zanzibar . . . pressing down on Africa.

I was in a near stupor by the time Seyyid introduced me to the slave market. Didn't want to connect the sight to my brain. Had to. Naked black Africans were chained up worse than animals. Hundreds of them, herded together on the hard-packed dirt under the eagle eyes and whips of more fierce Arabs. I stared at the swirls scarred into the men's backs, onto the women's breasts . . . at the sheer hopelessness on the faces streaming sweat under the merciless sun. Could've bought Hannah her black baby here for sure. I studied a few suckling from their mother's teats: their limbs withered sticks, letting out whining mewls, as if their mums' milk'd gone dry. The sight brought on cramps near worse than my first seasick days. Maybe that fiery stew sauce contributed. Still and all . . . . Clutching my stomach, I turned to Seyyid.

"See, boss?" He pointed with pride. "Sheikhs buy for harem slaves. Worth many shillings, many rupees."

I reached in my pocket for the coins I'd promised for his services. Added a few extra. Wasn't his fault he was born here. "Go home, Seyyid. I've seen enough of Zanzibar."

"But, boss—"

The cramps ratcheted up. Who knew that separating day-dreams from reality could be so painful? "Bugger off!"

Grasping my parcels, I stumbled back to where I'd forsaken my donkeys. Wishing for their innocence, I collapsed under the

27

shade of a palm tree next to the dozing Abdullah and Hamid. The heat of the afternoon wore on.

When we left Zanzibar on a southbound ship, the *Madura*, it was with a different kind of livestock. Stanley had squeezed 620 porters for the Congo into the bowels of the vessel. Two hours out of port I discovered they weren't all Zanzibaris. A good number happened to be Soudanese from the desert country south of Egypt, and they didn't much care for each other. As I glanced down the hatchway, wondering how on earth they'd all fit between decks abreast of the baking heat of the boilers, a ruckus broke out. The men massed into Soudanese and Zanzibari mobs, and firewood started flying across the divide. Fistfights soon followed. The Soudanese were much taller. Faster, too. They seemed to have the advantage. Then blood began to flow.

"Mr. Stanley!" I yelped.

He was already trotting across the main deck. Peering down into the half light. "Officers!" he roared.

I hastily cleared a path for Barttelot & Company—the *Company* having increased with the additions of Messrs. John Rose Troup, William Bonny, and James Sligo Jameson in Suez. Watched them all descend into the depths with Stanley following. Only then did I edge closer to follow the action.

Stanley and his men were a tiny white wedge within a black sea of faces, yet they attacked with complete confidence, even glee. Whips, sticks—they bore down on the porters with all the enthusiasm of Abdullah and Hamid in league against my stubborn donkeys. I suddenly knew. Beasts of burden. For Stanley and his elect, these Africans were naught but beasts of burden.

There was a rung on the social ladder lower than mine.

"Good shindy, men!" Stanley called.

Cries rose to Allah. Heads cracked like melons.

"Ho, Nelson!" Stanley again. "Bravo, Jephson!"

I pulled away, grateful for once I wasn't numbered among Henry Morton Stanley's *officers*. At dusk I hovered unseen in the long shadows of the funnels, watching as a handful of robe-wrapped bodies were slung overboard into the warm currents of the Indian Ocean.

Finally I got to do some quartermastering work—but then so did near everyone else on the expedition—always excepting Tippu-Tib, who'd also joined us in Zanzibar and was currently lolling about with his wives and entourage in first-class comfort. He was known as the King of the Slavers, a black Arab wrapped in a crisp white turban and robes as meticulously kept as Stanley's uniforms. His full graying beard decorated with braids caught your attention first; then the broad nose he claimed from his Bantu "princess" mother; finally, the shrewd eyes. Seems Stanley'd made a devil's deal with the slaver to round up more manpower for us once we reached the Congo. Less said about *all* of that.

The second morning out from Zanzibar I stood with the rest of the European expedition members gathered above decks at Stanley's command. Jauntily sporting a pith helmet he'd picked up in Zanzibar, he paraded before us, lecturing in his flat American twang. It was a fair trial holding back my grin as Barttelot & Company were assigned to labor in tandem with me. 'Course, being unused to the very idea of *real* work, it took them a little longer to figure out the way the wind blew. Stanley took his time leading up to it, too.

"Right, men. Here's the drill. Our mission is to transport sufficient ammunition to the Emin Pasha to enable him to withdraw from his dangerous position. Prime Minister Nubar Pasha of Egypt has kindly allowed us to carry the Egyptian colors for the duration since the Emin's province of Equatoria is claimed by Egypt . . . which—as you're perfectly aware—is currently under Great Britain's wing. We're also expected to withdraw with the Emin Pasha's seventy-five-odd tons of ivory—"

"I say," Barttelot interrupted. "We're talking about sixty thousand quids' worth!"

Stanley snapped his whip in annoyance. "Precisely. A fortune.

A percentage of which the prime minister has promised to the expedition to help defray our current expenses."

He tapped his helmet's brim against the rising sun.

"Thus the equation is simple. Ammunition in, ivory out—along with the Emin Pasha and his staff, of course." He cleared his throat. "Now then. A porter can carry a maximum of seventy pounds, exclusive of his own kit. The task at hand between here and Cape Town is to divide the stores of ammunition acquired in Zanzibar into seventy-pound parcels. After which the expedition's provisions and trade goods must be similarly apportioned. Do I make myself clear?"

Captain Nelson tapped his swagger stick on the deck for attention. "Am I to properly understand that your officers are to undertake this manual labor of weighing and packing?"

"Correct!" Stanley snapped. "You may use the Zanzibaris for hauling commodities between decks, but the Soudanese *askaris* are soldiers by birthright and consider themselves to be expedition guards. They'd kill you sooner than dirty their hands."

"Excuse me, Mr. Stanley." This time the youngish Jephson interrupted in his annoyingly high-pitched voice. "But the numbers don't add up. If the Soudanese among our six hundred-odd men are meant to be guards, surely we'll be far short of porters—"

"Matadi, Jephson. We will take on more porters in Matadi from the Congo Free Staters. They are far easier to find than men to guard our critical supplies."

He proper glared at the man, then turned to hone in on *me*. I near quaked under his piercing eyes.

"Regarding these critical supplies, never forget: 'Some things are best left in guaranteed honest hands.' Rifle cartridges happen to be the most favored form of currency in the Congo. It wouldn't behoove us to allow the ammunition to be siphoned off by the porters for barter—or for unauthorized use in our stock of Remingtons . . . would it?"

Stanley disappeared, leaving that question floating.

"Well done, Jephson," Lieutenant Stairs drawled.

"It's hardly my fault," Jephson whined. "I wouldn't be making an ass of myself with questions if the old man didn't insist on keeping his plans so close to the chest."

At which point Mr. William Bonny, who'd escorted Baruti to the Suez—a no-nonsense, four-square ex-soldier built like a mastiff—took over as drill sergeant.

"First things first," he roared. "Ormsby—locate the Expedition's scales. Nelson—organize the Zanzibaris into relay teams from the hold to the main deck. Barttelot—"

We worked from dawn to dusk beneath the hot sun. Measuring the loads down to the ounce. Packaging and labeling them. Restacking the goods in the hold under the watchful eye of Soudanese guards. The only diversion came several mornings later. That's when T. H. Parke—the expedition's surgeon who'd been recruited by Stanley in Cairo and had managed to excuse himself from the current chores—arrived mid ship with a stool in one hand and a leather carryall in the other. Following him was a box-bearing galley steward and two seamen lugging canvas and poles.

"Where'll you be wantin' your shade, Doc?" asked one of the sailors.

Parke carefully placed his stool on deck, regally sat upon it, and gestured. "Directly over me, if you please."

All progress halted as we watched the men construct a tent above and around T. H. Parke. I wiped sweat from my brow, then forgot about the heat as the steward deposited his box—and, inexplicably, a gong and mallet—next to the surgeon. Parke, a rather dashing man with a regulation mustache and a promising spark of humor in his wide eyes, picked up the gong. He bashed it enthusiastically with the mallet, then listened to its reverberations with evident pleasure.

"Now hear this!"

He certainly had our attention. Fully.

"Henry Morton Stanley has decreed that every member of his Expedition for the Relief of Emin Pasha shall be vaccinated—"

"For the smallpox?" I blurted out. "How? The vaccine needs to be kept cold, else it loses its effectiveness!"

"Observant of you, Ormsby. It is Ormsby?"

I nodded.

"Take note." He pointed to the box. "Enough doses to cure half of Africa of the scourge, carefully kept on ice by Mr. Stanley himself out from London." He paused to smile with satisfaction. "And by yours truly from Cairo to Suez to these very decks. As you're such an expert, young Ormsby, you may dispense with your plebeian labors and assist me in my nobler work."

Under the shade. Thank you, Burroughs & Wellcome.

"With pleasure, sir." I trotted forward.

"Remove your shirt, please."

"Why?"

"You shall have the pleasure of receiving the first vaccination."

"But I've already received it, sir. As a lad. It's required by law in England, after all." In proof of which, I yanked off my sweat-sodden shirt and displayed the evidence on my upper arm. "There's the scar, regulation ha'penny size."

"No matter. Everyone is to be vaccinated."

"Even the porters?" I asked in disbelief.

"Especially the porters. What if they were to suddenly expire of smallpox in the midst of some ungodly jungle?"

Should've known Stanley wasn't that much of a humanitarian. Got to get that ivory out of the bush. Still, best of motives or not, you couldn't argue with trying to wipe out smallpox. With a sigh I presented my other arm. "Might as well match 'em up."

Surgeon Parke grinned. "Indeed."

After the grumbling expedition members were duly re-vaccinated, it became my duty to bang the gong. When a sufficient number of Zanzibaris had presented themselves—a sufficient number of Soudanese had, too, but they hovered suspiciously at the edges of the throng—Surgeon Parke gave a little speech which was translated phrase by phrase into Swahili and Arabic by the linguists among the porters. It went something like this: "In his great wisdom, your white father Bula Matari—"

That's what the Africans called Stanley, loosely meaning "the Smasher of Rocks," which was beginning to make sense to me.

"—has decreed that you be given medicine. It is a wonderful medicine that will save you from the pox that leaves faces filled with holes like boulders. It is a wonderful medicine that will give you strength to live long years without death from the sickness that comes with the running holes. It is a gift he gives freely. Who shall receive it first?"

Well, there was a fair amount of shuffling. It looked as if it would go on for a long time. A very long time.

"With your leave?" I said to the surgeon. He raised an eyebrow, but nodded. I picked up the gong and gave it another whack. Then I left the shelter of the awning, still shirtless, to boldly face the throng.

"Look upon me, brothers."

I flexed my newly acquired biceps—the biceps Burroughs & Wellcome couldn't have offered me in fifty years. I pointed to the old vaccination scar, then to the rapidly reddening new one. Made sure all the gawkers had a good look. As they shoved forward, I had a sudden flash of the medicine witch, Gulai, back in Zanzibar. The wild hair . . . the fierce scars . . . those eyes. Still had the power to make me shiver through the heat, Gulai did. Suspecting these men lived with the selfsame superstitions, I laid it on.

"I have received this magic medicine, better than any talisman, *two* times. It makes me strong as a bull." Another flex of the muscles, followed by a broad wink. "In *many* ways," I added, to emphasize the point. I waited for the translation to filter through the crowd. Waited for the knowing pokes and rumbling chuckles. Plunged back in. "A *real* man never need fear it!"

Folding my arms, I bided my time under the scorching sun. More shuffling. Finally one of the Zanzibari translators stepped forward.

He pounded his chest. "I, Tewfik, am a man. I will be bold."

I scuttled back under the awning and handed Surgeon Parke one of the special split-tip needles from the carryall. Opened another vial of vaccine. Gestured to the volunteer to present an arm. He boldly yanked off his robe and thrust his right arm forward . . . then pulled it back. "It will give scar?"

I darted a look at Parke. He hesitated, then, "Er . . . usually—"

"Good."

Back came the arm. Parke poked it with the needle and daubed on the vaccine. Tewfik the Bold swaggered away, flourishing his arm. What followed was a near riot as his fellows fought to be next. Barttelot & Company were forced to drop their work to organize a queue. The inoculations proceeded at a record pace.

Barely wrapping up the vaccination job late the next day, the porters began re-gathering. Parke looked at me. "What now?"

Tewfik stepped forward once more. Ripped off his *dishdash*. Presented his unvaccinated arm. "I wish to be decorated two times. Others wish it, too." He pointed at me. "Just as Bull Boy."

I groaned.

Surgeon Parke choked but managed to control his laughter. "I'll let you handle this one, Bull Boy."

Brought this upon my own head fair and square.

With a sigh I grabbed the gong, then snatched the stool from beneath Parke. Mounting it before the tent in full sight of all, I whacked a mighty ringing blow upon the gong. Waited for the reverberations to stop bouncing through my head. Took a deep breath and addressed the porters.

"Greetings again, brothers. You are wise in your desires. Such a scar is a fine charm, indeed. Alas, the magic medicine is all gone. Finished. There is no more to be had—but from far, far away in England, where the glorious Queen Victoria makes it for you."

A pause while this was digested, then, "Be brave, my brothers! You must wait for Bula Matari's next expedition to receive your second scar. Until then, the new magic within you will be strong enough for all your needs." Another broad wink. "Strong enough to make your wives very happy when you return to them after the rescue of Emin Pasha—strong enough to make fine new sons to sit by your fires."

The porters cheered as Bull Boy descended from his pulpit with as much dignity as could be mustered. A satisfied congregation is always a good thing. Yet the thought crossed my mind that this was not exactly the sort of witnessing Pastor Gribbins'd had in mind when he'd last prayed over me.

There followed more days of weighing and packing under the hot sun. Nights filled first with soothing Arabic prayers, then with the soulful songs and drums of our Zanzibaris. Their music flowed from the hold, enveloping the ship, spreading out over the Indian Ocean—back to Zanzibar, ahead to the unknown.

When the *Madura* rounded the Cape of Good Hope at last, she dropped anchor within the green and flowered shelter of Cape Town. This time I rode the launch to shore next to the mailbag with the latest batch of my letters for home. Surgeon Parke had invited me to join him in seeing the sights.

We wandered the wharfside pubs, admired the old fortress, then struck off by carriage for Table Mountain—hovering like a vast, flat monument over all. When the rough track ended halfway up, we abandoned the carriage to scale its heights by foot. It was a sheer pleasure to stretch my legs after the weeks aboard ship. A sheer pleasure to laugh at the fat, groundhog-like dassies—a kind of hyrax, Doc claimed—that popped up among the rocks, scolding at our approach. And at the top . . . at the top of Table Mountain was a view of tiny ships at anchor within their safe harbor. Beyond lay the foot of the entire continent of Africa—and the sea lay beyond that, running straight to the frozen shores of Antarctica.

"Past compare, eh, old chap?" Parke lounged against a boulder, puffing contentedly on a cigar.

"For a cert!"

I spread my arms and gathered it in.

THE CONGO

MARCH 18, 1887, IT WAS. STILL IN THE GOLDEN
Jubilee Year of Victoria in some different world, maybe on a whole
different planet. Anyhow, that's when the *Madura* entered the
steaming mouth of the Congo River. And there was me, Tom
Ormsby, having circumnavigated near the entire continent of
Africa. And survived, to boot.

I hung over the railing below the bridge watching the jungle
closing in, watching the ship drop anchor in the oily waters just off
a sandy point called Banana. There were no cheering crowds to
greet us, no flags flying—only two yellowish, dried up-looking
traders from the British Congo Company who tottered aboard,
sheltering from the sun under ladies' parasols. With Stanley
already disembarked and heading for the small station on land,
Barttelot & Company swarmed 'round these Englishmen to hear
the local news.

Famine in the country . . . villages along the road to Stanley Pool
deserted . . . every riverboat wrecked, rotten, or missing its boilers and
engines . . .

When Surgeon T. H. Parke slipped away from the doomsayers,

I decided to do the same. He gave me a wry smile. "Notice how grim tidings are always offered with the greatest glee? What say we commandeer a boat and assay this country for ourselves? Let Stanley sort out the mess."

Finally, I'd set foot in *The Deepest Darkest Congo*.

"Lead the way, Doc!"

T. H. Parke and I left the launch's sailors doing a wild mosquito-slapping jig on the beach. The surgeon calmly lit a cigar and blew a cloud of smoky protection around us. "I'm for avoiding most of the settlement—"

"And Stanley's fury if he spots us away without leave?"

He grinned. "Precisely. Unlike my fellow officers, I'm not an ivory man. My interest in the Congo lies in the flora. I have a little theory about how the land holds the cure for its specific illnesses." A thoughtful puff on the cigar, a sigh at the whining black cloud of mosquitoes massing for an attack. "Truth be told, my purpose in signing on for the expedition was to collect as many specimens as possible. Ship them home for study—"

"I can help!" I blurted out. "You know I've apprenticed with chemists and have *some* feeling for medicine!"

Parke laughed. "After watching you rally the porters for their 'magic charms,' I suspect your talents lie closer to theater, Ormsby. But why not?"

We entered the forest jungle. It wasn't hard. A few steps from the beach, and we were enclosed by a Garden of Eden gone to mad wild tangles: mossy limbs reaching out, creeping vines stretching down, sinewy arms dangling . . . arms? With fingers?

I brushed a cobweb from my face. "Um, Doc?"

Too late. Before my eyes a furry hand snatched his cap. Slack-jawed, I watched the cap's progress as its jaunty red checks popped in and out of the green canopy overhead. I finally had the sense to spit out a mouthful of buzzing insects and clamp my jaw shut.

"What the dickens—"

Parke broke into a stumbling run over roots grown the perfect size for tripping. I followed him. We both followed the—

"Monkey!" he exclaimed as we broke through to a clearing.

We stared up at the rascal hanging by his tail at the jungle's edge. Flipping the bright cap. Taunting us.

"'Pon my word, I hadn't taken the fauna into account." Parke grabbed a stick and flung it at the thief. Bull's-eye! Chattering with anger, the creature hurled the cap back at him. He bent for it, then glanced around. "What in the world . . ."

I'd just registered where we were standing. "Well out of it, I think."

We'd landed in a hidden cemetery. Wooden crosses were lined in sagging rows, their painted memorials peeling and fading in the humidity that hovered like a concrete blanket over everything. I read one aloud. "K. A. Kieman, born 1864. Died . . ." The date was lost . . . . "Say, he was only six years older than me!"

Parke gave me a sharp look, then examined other markers. "All of them out from England. All of them dead before their twenty-fifth birthday."

Stanley's one in three.

I took in the plots again, swallowed some of the fetid air, stared at the bloody remnants of mosquitoes smashed on my arms. Re-assessed. Only a fraction of Stanley's one in three. The Congo would hold other hidden graves. The Relief of Emin Pasha Expedition would add more.

Surgeon T. H. Parke fiddled with the cap in his hands, then made a little bow to the dead. Clapping the hat firmly on his head, he turned to me. "But we're made of sterner stuff, eh, Bull Boy?"

That's when I buried Jack Harkaway. Right next to these poor blighters.

"Pray Heaven."

By the next day Stanley had rounded up three "nonexistent" steamboats. Under the attentions of Mr. John Walker—a steamboat engineer we'd picked up in Cape Town—these took our expedition the 120 miles up the Congo River to Matadi, where the river's rapids made navigation impossible for the next 200 miles to Stanley Pool. We debarked at Matadi on the twenty-first of March. On the twenty-second, Stanley sent an advance party of porters to organize food caches along the expedition's route. By the twenty-third, he'd rounded up another 220 porters. On the twenty-fifth, the remainder of the party was scheduled to set off.

Me, too. Tom Ormsby: apprentice engine mate, donkey keeper, surgeon's assistant, future botanist, general all-round dogsbody, and one chap freshly in awe of Henry Morton Stanley. For a cert, he was a swaggering, bullying little Napoleon. But the man got results.

Matadi at the head of the Congo rapids, March 25. The trumpets sounded their wake-up calls at 5:15 AM. By 6:00 AM the porters and *askaris* had offered their morning prayers, tents were folded, and companies of Zanzibaris had been organized by captains and Soudanese guards. At 6:15 AM sharp, the main body of the Relief of Emin Pasha Expedition was marching single file in chanting rhythm to Stanley Pool. Stanley himself was in the vanguard with Tippu-Tib, the king of the slavers, and his entire entourage of wives and retainers. The porters carried their seventy-pound allotments of ammunition, their nine-pound rifles, and four days' rations of rice, all on top of their own kit of clothing and bedding mats. I carried my nine-pound rifle—the same single-shot Remington that'd been issued to everyone—a cartridge pouch strapped 'round my waist, and a water canteen. Within two hours, the robust chants had disappeared. Wet heat had all of us soggy to the core and near to dropping like flies.

Bloody misery.

This two hundred-mile journey to Stanley Pool wouldn't ever—couldn't ever—be the "short walk" I'd described to Mum.

I'd been randomly placed in charge—the "father," as Stanley put

it—of the column of porters captained by Tewfik the Bold of vaccination fame. He was tall for a Zanzibari—near as tall as the
Soudanese—which put us pretty much eye-to-eye with each
other. Must've been near Stanley's age, for his close-cropped hair
was grizzled and receded under his turban. His nose stood out,
too, but not like those of the fierce Arabs I'd seen earlier. It had
the slimness of the Abyssinians who'd been part of Zanzibar's
international crowds. He also sported a neat little chin beard,
befitting his position of authority.

Here was a man proud, experienced, and my elder. Was I to
look upon him as my "child"? To treat his men as my "children?"

How bleeding patronizing could you get?

Yet proud or not, like every porter he bowed, scraped, and
near flinched before Stanley's officers. But not before me.
Somehow Tewfik had decided I was his bosom mate. I hadn't had
time to sort out where that put me on the expedition's social ladder, but didn't give a fig. Could be, I'd been blessed with an ally.

"Bull Boy," he began, as we tramped in unison on our third
morning out. "Take heart, brother. Only *tisa*, nine, of my
Zanzibaris have gone to their reward in the Gardens of Allah."

"Died? Since we began the march?"

A careless nod. He was busy muttering, "*moja, mbili, tatu,*" as
he made calculations on his fingers. "Only this many—"

I counted *tatu*, three fists, and *mbili*, two fingers. "Seventeen?"

"It is so. Only *seven-teen* abandoned this morning. From sickness."

Only? "But Tewfik—"

He waved off my protest. "Magic medicine cannot help for
now. This I know. From other marches. We grow soft from boat.
Soft from much food. In one month all will be well. All will be—"

"Acclimated?" I tried.

He stumbled on rubble and grabbed for the shifting load balanced on his head. "Worn to the work. You, too."

"But I carry nothing but my rifle!" It was my turn to stumble.
The "road" was a narrow path Stanley'd blasted from the rock ten

years back, giving him his honorary nickname of Bula Matari. Now the path rose uphill, carved between a solid wall of grasping vegetation and the cliffs hulking over the Congo River raging below. It wouldn't do to slip and fall into those rapids. I righted myself. "You shame me, brother."

Tewfik gazed on the long line of carriers wobbling ahead of us before they disappeared over the rise. "It is the black man's burden."

"Not for always!" I fumed.

"*Inshallah*, may you speak the truth."

God willing. How curious it would be to have the tables turned. Yet not under Stanley's rule.

Acclimation was proceeding at a snail's pace. Porters swooned and fell up and down the endless road. One moment a man would be balancing a load upon his back or head. The next, his knees would crumple. With barely a sigh, he'd sway off the path and sprawl among his burdens. On marched the columns, ants focused only on their nest beyond, leaving the stricken to rally or die, as Allah willed.

The first time I saw this happen, I stopped to give aid. Wouldn't any civilized Christian? I'd gotten as far as finding the man's gourd and splashing water into his mouth, when—

"Ormsby!"

A vicious kick knocked the gourd from my grasp. As I reached for it, a boot pinned my hand flat. I watched the earth swallow the gourd's precious liquid, then looked up. Stanley's martinet sergeant.

"Mr. Bonny."

He shook his furled whip. "*Never* leave your column."

"But this man needs help!"

"The black sluggard can recover and catch up on his own time." Bonny's heel ground into my hand. "*Never* abandon your command. Understood?"

"Yes, sir. Perfectly."

He raised his boot, and I cradled my bruised hand back to my command.

Hell's bones. Stanley's men had as little mercy for me as for their "children."

The "black sluggards" kept right on collapsing. So on the fourth day we camped at noon to avoid the worst killing hours of heat. I had a sneaking suspicion that giving the porters a rest wasn't due to Christian charity; more likely, to keep them from expiring in droves. Was a limit to the manpower available, wasn't there? At any rate, Stanley chose a site called Congo la Lemba. Soon cook fires surrounded by listless porters flared at the edges of the clearing. Zanzibaris barricaded themselves behind their heaped packs on the western side, Soudanese behind their tripods of rifles on the east.

Silly blighters. Still can't stand each other. Even when all of 'em drop everything to pray to Allah five times a day. Then again, the Golden Rule of loving your neighbor didn't seem like the strong point of this expedition, either.

The center of camp was always reserved for the tents of Stanley and his expedition officers. Naturally. I wandered past crews raising the canvas, then through a stretch of tall grass, toward a scraggly orchard of guava, palm, and lemon trees choked with reeds. Parke was standing nearby, thoughtfully puffing on a cigar.

"Ormsby." He nodded. "Hard to believe, eh?"

"What?"

"The last time Stanley was here, ten years back, this was a thriving village. Seems its chief got a little cheeky with the caravans passing through. Started demanding tolls."

I knew this story didn't have a happy ending, but I had to ask. "And?"

"Insolence, eh? One can't put up with insolence and run a

new country. The Congo Free State's mercenaries, the *Force Publique*, hired a notorious local tribe called the Bangalas to behead the chief and torch his village."

"What happened to the rest of the people?"

Parke shrugged. "If they survived the standard rape and pillage, they certainly didn't stick around for more. Especially since the Bangalas seem to have a taste for human flesh."

"Cannibalism?" My skin prickled down to my toes, quite a different sort of prickle from the heat rash I'd been living with.

It wasn't one of McNabb's tall tales. Cannibalism truly existed.

"There seems to be a certain amount of it going around. It's quite useful for intimidation. Makes the next few villages think twice about getting uppity, eh? Given the choice between cooperation or being eaten—"

"But . . ." I fought off a sudden seizure of those Zanzibar cramps. "Shouldn't it be the other way 'round? The authorities protecting the natives?"

"Tom, Tom." Doc dragged on his cigar. Exhaled. "King Leopold of Belgium *personally* owns the Congo Free State. Stanley pretty much handed it to him on a platter after his last expedition—aside from the pitiful British concessions at the Congo's mouth." He gestured around. "Everything on our side of the Congo River belongs to Leopold. The French sucked up a good piece of the opposite side. Leopold also owns the *Force Publique*, his personal police force."

"And they aren't exactly here for training the natives to set up a proper government, are they?"

Parke snorted. "A proper colonial government? You were expecting schools, and literacy, and the odd hospital clinic popping up in the bush? When there's ivory and rubber to be taken? Wake up. It's all about politics and money. Mainly money."

Blistering Hell. And the natives be damned.

I studied the charred remains of huts beneath the tall grass. Neat little rectangles, they were. I kicked a burned pole in frustration. The most horrific beetles and centipedes scurried out. I scurried, too. To a safe distance. "When do we see this *Force Publique?*" Like to know what a soulless mercenary looked like.

"Not to worry. There'll be more than you'd care to meet in Leopoldville, when we get to Stanley Pool."

The bugs were still scuttling mindlessly. I stared at them in fascination. So bleeding ugly. Kind of matched the country. Which reminded me. "About your flora—"

Parke eyed the thick bush beyond the clearing. "Another day, I think. When we're well out of Bangala territory."

Not that I'd seen any real natives yet. Only abandoned villages. Like those English traders back in Banana had warned us. Was it because of famine? Or fear of the Bangala? The questions kept my mind working during the endless treks. Kind of kept my feet moving, too, not knowing if arrows or spears or cook pots might poke through the bush of scruffy low trees when we angled off from the river. But the only things poking out were troops of thieving monkeys. Baboons, too, much bigger and nastier . . . and then a *warthog.*

"Bleeding—" I froze. "What's that?"

"*Ngiri.*" Tewfik spat. "*Swine.* An eater of offal. Forbidden meat."

Never had I seen a pig like this one. Four times the size of an English boar, he seemed. I stared at the snorting, pawing creature who'd broken through the bush just ahead. Looked like he'd been surprised by us, too, because he lowered his head and postured with his curved tusks most ferociously. I laughed. He was wickedly homely—that snout, the ferocious scowl furrowing his forehead, the tufts of bristles sticking up worse than my cowlick.

"He's wonderful!" I cried. "He's—"

Shots rang out.

"Supper!" Barttelot crowed.

It never crossed my mind that we'd meet anyone on this god-awful "road" of Stanley's, but the next day a Mr. Herbert Ward popped out of the bush. Stanley hailed him like an old friend and prompt-ly hired him. It seemed the man had worked for Stanley on his last expedition and more recently for the Congo Free State. When French traders appeared next, I realized this was the *only* trade route currently available on either the Belgian or French sides of the Congo River.

The French caravan carried about three hundred elephants' worth of tusks, by my count. Never thought there'd be that many elephants in the entire world. But they weren't in it anymore, were they? Then it began to rain—if that's what you'd call it. God's truth, England never saw its equal. Like a burst dam it fell, shat-tering everyone's nerves, turning the road into a sticky bog that clung to my boots and trousers, making every new step a squish-ing agony. I'll say this for it, though. That rain finally taught me the meaning of commanding a column.

We were slogging along, trying to catch up with Stanley's front column, several weeks into our acclimating. Night was falling too fast. It did that out here in Africa. One minute, the sun would be setting, a reddish-golden globe at our backs. The next—total, impenetrable blackness. No endless twilight like back home. No chance of getting adjusted to the close of day. Scary, it was. *Worse* in the merciless downpour that gave no hint that night was crash-ing down. Queer sounds everywhere . . . beasts I'd never seen, so couldn't half imagine how big their teeth might be—or their appetites. Monkey howls and watery bird screeches—

"Ai-yeeeeeeeeee!"

I plowed into Tewfik. "That wasn't an animal!"

Tewfik the Bold froze, babbling prayers to Allah. I peered through the deluge and fast-disappearing half-light as the cry came again.

"Bloody Hell!"

I fought my way back down our column. The porters had piled into each other in the middle of the mucky path, silently watching two human shapes making a good try at throttling each other to death.

"**Enough of that!**" I bellowed.

Might as well've been tongueless and dumb for all the mind they paid. Groping for a cartridge, I blindly loaded my rifle. Aimed it at the stormy sky. Pulled the trigger. As the explosion cracked through the rain, the figures broke apart. I marched up to glare at them, Zanzibari and Soudanese both.

"Explain yourselves!" I barked. "The road is not hard enough? The falling rain is not torture enough? Your packs are not heavy enough?"

The gunshot must've jolted Tewfik into usefulness, because suddenly he was behind me, translating. When he paused, the great brute of a Soudanese made himself taller. "This dog of a Zanzibari,"—he spat —"dared *touch* me."

The Zanzibari in question—half his size—was doubled over, clutching his neck and gasping for breath.

"This is reason to strangle the man? For shame! Are we not all brothers fighting the road, fighting the heavens?"

The Soudanese sullenly draped his hood over his head and dropped his eyes. "It is as you say, *bwana kidogo.*"

Little Master. That I understood without translation. I sighed. "Get you to the rear for your patrol duty. Look no more on this man. His insult was not from the heart, but from weariness."

The villain stalked off, still full of himself. I shouldered the gun and turned to Tewfik. "Thank you for your help, my brother."

He shrugged. "*Mvua. Mno mvua.* Too much rain."

I swiped the *mvua* from my eyes and addressed the waiting porters: "Let us find our home for the night. We are all weary."

By the time I finally straggled into the tent I shared with Parke, nothing mattered but the bowl of stew he offered me. Sagging on the edge of my cot, I shoved a spoonful toward my mouth—

"Ormsby!"

Someone yanked open the flap of our tent. Thrust in his head. The lamplight magnified the carefully parted hair, the fastidiously trimmed and shaped mustache. Barttelot.

"Stanley's asking for you."

Parke lifted an eyebrow. I set down my supper and trudged back into the storm.

Stanley's tent was bigger. He had *two* lamps and a portable desk laid out with his writing tools. He was sitting before it in a camp chair, stretching out a hand for the mug of tea Baruti was bringing from a tiny paraffin stove. A mug of *steaming* tea I could've killed for.

"You wanted to see me, sir?" I dripped at attention.

He turned to face me. "I understand you had an incident in your column tonight, Ormsby."

Did the man have spies everywhere? "Only weather and weariness."

"And you dealt with it how?"

"A shot in the air to catch their attention, then a few words, sir."

"So far so good. And next?"

What next? "I separated the combatants and proceeded to camp, sir."

"Without meting out punishment?"

"We were all rather at the end of our tethers, sir. It would've hardly been useful—"

"Ormsby." He rose, scowling. "You are a white man. The men under your charge are black. It is necessary to retain your natural superiority. A show of force is essential to accomplish this end."

True weariness, bone weariness, near overcame me. "What would you have me do?"

"Flog the villains, of course. Both of them."

"But I haven't even got a whip!"

His scowl deepened. "That lack will be attended to in Leopoldville."

I tried backtracking from my error. "I don't think a whip will be necessary—"

"Ormsby. Consider the numbers. They are eight hundred. We are a dozen. Should mutiny rear its ugly head, where would we be?"

"Mutiny, sir? The men are just tired. Surely it's not an issue—"

"Not now!" he snapped. "When things get rougher."

Rougher?

"In holding a tight upper hand, perception is all, Ormsby. Keep that firmly in mind."

"Yes, sir."

He about-faced and sat at his desk again. "You are excused."

"Certainly, sir. Thank you, sir."

Bleeding agony.

I returned to the deluge, my cold stew, and my musty bed. None of them were improved by my "natural superiority."

THE RIVER CRUISE

STANLEY HAD A MEMORY LIKE AN ELEPHANT.
More's the pity. We'd barely arrived in Leopoldville at the end of
our two hundred-mile march when I was presented with my very
own *chicote*—the snarlingly superior *Force Publique* officers'
scourge of choice. The Congo Free State's official whip. This
chicote wasn't ever as clean or straightforward as a dog or horse
whip. Whipwise, it put your standard bullwhip—with its long
vicious lash—to shame, not to mention your cat-o'-nine-tails.
Invented by the first Portuguese slave traders, it had a thick
leather handle wrapped around five endless lashes of twisted
hippo hide. Nasty stuff, that hippo hide. The *chicote*? Just another
thing that matched the country . . . only I was expected to use it
on human beings.

    Bloody misery.

Next Stanley mustered the entire expedition just outside the town
to make an inventory of carriers and goods that'd actually arrived
in Leopoldville. I helped, ticking off my lists as if I were still in the
stockroom of Burroughs & Wellcome. But instead of bottle-filled

shelves, I was itemizing long columns of men sweltering under the blistering equatorial sun. And instead of listening to old Crockett slurp his tea, I heard the roar of the Ntame Rapids below us. I chanced a look over the cliff . . . to just beyond the rapids, where pools were filled with half-submerged hippos, not to mention crocodiles long enough and sharp-toothed enough to swallow the entire Relief of Emin Pasha Expedition.

I'd have to write Mum and the girls about all this. It would be the last letter I could get off to them before we took to the next round of steamboats. There's no telling when I'd have another chance. Maybe even add a little sketch. Make the crocs smile, the way they looked when they spread their toothy jaws for the kill. Then Hannah could laugh, 'stead of getting nightmares from imagining them.

The spume from the rapids held me hypnotized, and I found myself counting hippos. Stopped at thirty-three. Sure hoped the presents I'd sent from Zanzibar and Cape Town had made it home . . . along with my scimitar, too.

"Ormsby!"

I spun away from the cliff. "Mr. Stanley, sir?"

"Report your column's statistics. If you've finished sightseeing."

"Yes, sir. Certainly, sir." Coloring all the way up to my sunburned brow, I focused on the crumpled sheet in my hand. Rattled down the list. Stanley made a few notes, nodded, and finally excused the whole group.

Bleeding close call.

I swiped the sweat of embarrassment from my face and trotted off in the direction of the marketplace to purchase something new: a hat with a brim. A hat to shadow my embarrassments. A hat to cut the killing sun, too. Keep on squinting through it like I'd been, I'd end up as furrowed as that late lamented warthog.

"Ormsby!"

This time it was Lieutenant Stairs. "Sir?"

"Forgotten something, have you?"

I checked my person. Ever-present Remington . . . bulging cartridge pouch . . .

"Your whip." He sighed.

"Oh, er . . . thank you, sir."

I made tracks for where I'd abandoned it by the cliff. A pure shame I hadn't nudged it off the edge. Maybe it wasn't too late to do the deed. I peered over the drop to reconsider, but got distracted again by all those hippos. There were enough in that pool to feed half the Congo. If the local people were so hungry, why hadn't they gone after them? Could be those waiting crocs. And even if someone succeeded in bagging a few, how on earth would he save them from the crocs?

"The whip, Ormsby."

Bloody Hell. Stuck with it.

I reached for the handle and gave it an angry flick.

Lieutenant Stairs chuckled. "You need a little work on the wrist action, Ormsby."

The expedition's itinerary next featured that "pleasant steamboat cruise" up the Congo I'd mentioned to Mum way back in January. All 1,100 miles of it to someplace called Yambuya at the juncture of the Aruwimi River. That's where we would set off cross country, closing in on Emin Pasha at last. But first off, Stanley had to beg, borrow, and almost steal some more steamboats, since the first batch we'd used navigated only the lower Congo before the rapids began at Matadi.

We ended up with a collection that would've made Chief Engineer Alexander McNabb gag: the *Stanley*, the *Henry Reed*, and the *Peace*, broken-down claptraps all—along with their crews. And then there was the barely built *Florida*. She had no engine guts whatever since they hadn't been hauled up from Matadi yet, so she was demoted to a barge that the *Stanley* would tow. The *Florida* was a sweet-looking barge, though, with her pretty awnings and fretwork railings. We had to launch her from Kinshasa, twelve miles north of Leopoldville along the shores of Stanley Pool. It was during this march that I figured out that Stanley Pool was naught but a huge lake made by the Congo River spreading around a bunch of islands.

At Kinshasa, the expedition staff gathered under huge baobab trees to watch about two hundred Zanzibaris launch the *Florida* from her slip. As the cheers evaporated into the heat, we kept on squatting in the shade sweating the usual rivers. Meanwhile Stanley, freshly shaven and pressed by Baruti—did the man even know how to sweat?—paced before us in his immaculate whites. Wonder of wonders, he'd decided to share some of his problems.

"Gentlemen. Our recent mustering has brought a few pertinent statistics to light. Namely: we are short fifty-seven men and thirty-eight Remington rifles. Our actual count now is seven hundred thirty-seven men and four hundred ninety-six rifles. Of billhooks, axes, shovels, canteens, etc., we have lost over fifty percent. . . ."

Pertinent statistics? *Hell's bones.* The man was tallying up disaster. All those porters and supplies missing in only a twenty-eight-day march? Where'd they gotten to?

Stanley informed us.

It seems the porters were either dead from failing to acclimate fast enough, or were "bounty men" who'd accepted the four-month advance on their wages in Zanzibar with intentions of deserting at the first opportunity. As for the supplies, well, the Zanzibaris and Soudanese had bartered them for food from the villagers we'd encountered in the last week or so. Why? Rations were short and the men were hungry. Stanley stopped. Caught me with those fierce gray eyes.

"Ormsby."

I sprang to attention. "Sir."

"Your column had the least casualties, the least defections, the lowest rate of pilferage. Would you care to share the secret of your success with the rest of us?"

Sweat dribbled down my spine, drop by drop, as Barttelot & Company skewered me with looks, making me feel like one of those Giant Madagascar Hissing Cockroaches helplessly sizzling on a Zanzibar grill. I shook off the sensation. "Only interest in my men, sir. Treating them like human beings."

Amid general hilarity, Stanley nodded me down with, "Well done, Ormsby."

Fact is, it was that murderous Soudanese who'd set me straight. That and the onset of the rainy season. Or maybe I'd finally become acclimated. Instead of just trudging next to Tewfik, I'd begun walking the column, really looking at the men. Learning their names. Returning to Tewfik for their stories. They were mostly from Zanzibar's clove and cinnamon plantations. Some were free men, others escaped slaves and convicts. All were taking a chance at what could be good wages—if they survived—and a better life.

By Heaven, none of them were just numbers.

Then I started carrying a water bag in the heat of the day, sharing it as we marched. Began picking up a little more Swahili. The last week before Leopoldville I took to wandering through their night camps, seeing their pitiful rations. How could a man march with all that weight on his back on one pound of rice a day? When we stopped in the next village, I liberated a few handfuls of trade beads, and a few bundles of the copper wire used for money in the bush. Bartered it for bananas and Indian corn. Shared the bounty 'round Tewfik's campfires . . .

"Ormsby—"

I near hopped up again like a rabbit till I caught on that Stanley was assigning staff to steamboats.

"—the *Stanley*. Parke, the *Stanley*. Stairs—"

I stopped listening. Good. Maybe the doc and I could finally hunt for that flora of his.

Stanley cleared his throat.

"In light of our current situation, I'm afraid we'll have to leave a good portion of our supplies in storage in Leopoldville. There's not going to be enough room on these boats." He forestalled the questioning looks on his officers' faces. "Never fear, we'll have the steamboats return for them after we disembark for the Great Forest at the juncture of the Aruwimi River." He raised a hand to cut off the low rumble of protest.

"Also due to our current situation, I'm inaugurating new procedures. Henceforth, each of you will be responsible for a daily inspection of your men's cartridge pouches. Sales of ammunition to natives or Arabs must be avoided at all costs." Another throat clearing. "From this point onward it might behoove us to avoid irritating the men by being too exacting or showing unnecessary fussiness—"

"I say!" Barttelot broke in. "Are we expected to put up with cheek from these bounders?"

"Not at all, not at all, yet . . ." Stanley removed his pith helmet and actually swabbed his forehead with a handkerchief. "Officers should remember that the men's labor is severe, their burdens heavy, the climate hot, and rations scanty at best. The *Force Publique* appears to have alienated the local tribes to the extent that the natives refuse to barter food as in the past, leaving us without the possibility of topping up supplies along our route as planned. Leaving us in potential famine conditions—"

"Sir!"

This time it was Mr. James Sligo Jameson interrupting. He was the big-game hunter who'd joined our party at Suez after paying a thousand pounds for the pleasure. He wasn't a military man but carried the same superior airs, which is why I'd been ignoring him. But his next words interested me.

"I'd love to have a go at these hippopotamuses. A few of them should feed the porters indefinitely!"

Stanley clapped his helmet back on. "Permission granted. Go at it with my blessing before we embark. Now, as to the new punishment code—" He sought out Barttelot. "Discipline must be

taught and enforced, true, but henceforth let the rule be three
pardons for one punishment."

Well, then chaos really broke loose. I forgot about hippo hunting entire, and just sat there grinning like an idiot. Looked like I
could retire my *chicote* for the foreseeable future.

For a cert, those first few days aboard the *Stanley* were almost like
a pleasure cruise. We steamed around and between the islands of
Stanley Pool, then on up the Congo. The towed *Florida*, filled with
Tippu-Tib and his entourage, gently rose and fell in our wake, the
music wafting from under its gay awnings adding to the festive
mood. I'd managed to have my column boarded with me, and not
even Major Barttelot—the unfortunate choice for the *Stanley's*
officer in command—could keep my men below deck.

Small wonder then, that Surgeon T. H. Parke and I lolled on
deck chairs watching the scenery pass by, like well-heeled tourists
on a Thomas Cook excursion. The mosquito and fly populations
were down, a pleasant breeze slipped beneath the protective
awning to cool us, and my body was beginning to relax from the
tensions of the long march. I lazily watched the flight of a fish
eagle overhead, then smiled at a family of hippos bursting through
the water's surface for air. Chuckled at the antics of stiff, stilt-
legged cranes and spoonbills in the marshy grasses beyond the
hippos. My *chicote* and rifle were stowed under my bunk, and
Africa was beginning to bewitch me.

I spied Tewfik leaning over the railing farther down the deck.
"Tewfik the Bold!" I called. "Come. Join us."

Parke gave me a startled look but didn't complain as the
Zanzibari captain edged closer and deferentially touched fingers to
his turbaned head, lips, and heart. "I can be of service, my brother?"

"Yes." I kicked the empty chair next to me. "Sit. Talk with us."

"No, no. I could not impose myself upon you and Babu
Parke."

Parke stirred and patted a pocket in search of a cigar. He

wasn't used to the honorific for doctor yet. "Not an imposition, old chap."

Tewfik shifted nervously. "But the Bwana Major . . ."

Parke scratched a match on his boot sole. "Having a siesta," he said, applying flame to cigar. A puff, then, "Having a sleep."

"Ah."

Tewfik sank into the chair. Adjusted his robes. Adjusted his body. Stretched his legs halfway to the railing and crossed his ankles, just like ours. "This is the proper way to be seated?"

I laughed. "Spot on." And to make him more comfortable, I asked, "What is today, Tewfik?"

"Today?" He considered. "The days, they fly into each other . . . yet . . . it is the first day, I think."

"*Moja.*" I said. "One."

Tewfik beamed. "My brother Bull Boy remembers! *Jumamosi,* this day is called."

"'Pon my soul, is this *Saturday* we're talking about?" asked Parke.

"In Swahili." I grinned.

"Fascinating. Let's have more, shall we?"

Just so, we whiled away the afternoon till I could feel the *Stanley*'s engines cutting back. She nudged her way into shore and dropped anchor for the night.

Parke sighed. "I'm afraid it's time for the firewood brigade, Tewfik. We've got to stock up on fuel to keep this beast running tomorrow. You want to round up your men for the drill?"

Tewfik leaped from his chair as if it were on fire. "At once, Babu Parke. Most excellently will I see that they perform their tasks!"

Parke lazed another moment before stretching his legs and rising. "Nice going, Ormsby. Want to place any bets on how fast they gather the wood tonight?"

I laughed. "In record time."

"Good. Then you may take charge of the operation." He flung

his latest cigar stub into the river. "I'm going to collect my spade and plant kit and do a little prospecting before sunset."

The rainy season had sorted itself out. Now there was a heavy downpour early in the morning and another about noon. The fireworks saved themselves for the evening. I glanced up from the piles of wood littering the shoreline as the first bolt of lightning cut through the sky. Violent clouds were massing, as per usual.

"Tewfik! Are your men all back from the bush?" He'd sent out fifty gatherers for scrub and dead wood. I was overseeing a dozen ax men, making certain sure they whacked the wood into the thirty-inch lengths required for the boilers.

He counted on his fingers. "Almost, my brother. Only Dedan and Bhoke are lacking."

Bhoke. The Zanzibari near strangled by the Soudanese. Another bolt of lightning lit Tewfik's face. "They come!"

"Keep your men moving! We've got to finish loading this wood before the heavens break loose!"

I watched the ranks of porters climbing up the gangplank, arms filled with fuel. As the thunder moved closer, I turned to stare into the blackened bush. Parke was still out there, hunting his specimens. Hadn't he heard the storm coming? On impulse, I raced past Tewfik and plunged into the darkness.

"Where do you go?" he cried after me.

"I search for Babu Parke!"

Nice work, Bull Boy. The blind searching for the lost.

I shoved a branch from my face. It wasn't near as bad as that first bit of jungle by Banana, more bush than jungle. But I should've had the sense to bring a torch. Should've—

Thunder boomed overhead. The rains came with it. I pushed on. Another bolt of lightning saved me from laming myself over a great fallen tree.

Flaming Hell.

Were those legs sticking out? I pushed forward for a closer

look. Beneath the freshly uprooted giant, still sizzling from the bolt that'd toppled it, was—

"Doc!" I fell to my knees. "Doc! Are you all right?" Idiot. How could he be all right? He was pinned under this monster. I stretched out on the ground and felt for his head. Found it! His brow was warm, but his eyes were shut. I squirmed back and tried heaving the tree from his body. Lunged with everything in me. No good. The trunk hadn't budged an inch. Wouldn't in a million years with only me doing the shoving. I stood with the rain drenching me. What to try next? I couldn't lose Parke. He was my only ally among the expedition's officers . . . maybe even a friend. He was also a decent human being.

Think. Can't go racing off half-cocked.

I swiped rain from my eyes. *Right, then. Have to mark the spot. Go for help.* I revolved slowly, trying to memorize the shapes of surrounding trees, trying to fix on other distinguishing elements, like that weird light bobbing through the woods . . . *weird light?* It closed in on me.

"Dedan, Bhoke," eased from me like a prayer. "*Abeid*, Jojo. Welcome!"

"Move, little brother." Dedan thrust his flickering torch at me. "This is men's work."

Together the Zanzibaris lifted that great trunk from Parke's body. Together they bore him through the forest to the boat.

After I'd settled him into his bunk and laid a cool cloth atop the nasty bump on his forehead, he woke.

"Tom?"

"Right here, Doc. Your sample kit, too. I might've lost the spade, though."

A wince of pain crossed his features. "I seem to have chosen the wrong expedition for gentlemanly botanizing. Less collecting in future, I think."

Thunder boomed and wild winds tossed the ship at its anchor as I struggled to unknot the mosquito net hooked to the low cabin ceiling. It came loose at last, and I draped it over him. Carefully tucked it in. "Get some rest, Doc. Things are bound to look brighter in the morning."

They did, if you were of a mind to ignore the usual dawn deluge. Like to Noah's flood, it was. But here was I safe and sound aboard ship, ambling under the awnings of the wet, deserted deck in search of the cabin boy and Parke's tea. A smug smile was still plastered on my face when the *Stanley* jolted—

Scraped . . .

Groaned . . .

Hissed . . .

Lurched to a grinding halt.

Whereupon my boots slid all the way to the railing. I grabbed for it, hanging on for dear life while I digested the peculiar new angle of the *Stanley*. More hissing from the stacks . . . before the steam dissolved into one long, low, pitiful lament from the ship's horn.

A moment of pure silence, after which all hell broke loose.

"Allah save us!"

"We have run aground!"

"On a reef!"

Terrified black faces. Major Barttelot storming toward the pilot's house, bawling, "Dash it all, who's the incompetent fool of a navigator? Where's the captain?"

Sighing, I scrabbled up the inclined deck to extend my sympathy to the doc for his delayed tea. I strapped him safely into his sloping bunk, then descended to the engine room. Wasn't aught else for me to do, was there?

Chief Engineer Charters was swearing up a storm in the cramped space below deck.

"Wasna enough to misread the charts. The idjits atop ne'er rang down to stop engines. Ay, an' now me boiler's blown, me second section's torn to shreds, and dommed rivets popping from out the hull like corks!"

I squished through the Congo water seeping through the holes. "Will you be needing another pair of hands, chief? I apprenticed aboard the *Navarino*. . . ."

He halted his lament to look me up and down. Ran a hand through his bristling beard. "That'd be wi' Alexander McNabb?"

"It would."

"Best Scotsman on the water—aside from me. Roll up yere sleeves, laddie."

When the *Peace* and Stanley himself arrived to fuss over the damage, Charters had worked out the fix. We'd already cut up some old sheet-iron oil drums and banged them into plates. It only remained to screw them into the outside hull. By this time all the engineers from our fleet were crowding the engine room, wading with odd slanted gaits through the hold's two feet of water.

"A wee bit o' patience will be called for," Mr. Walker of Cape Town and points north observed. "A delicate touch."

"Ay," Charters agreed. "A nicety o' touch. Punchin' new holes through the hull itself. Matchin' 'em up wi' the plate holes from the outside—"

"Never forgettin' a good, clever diver to be holdin' up that outside plate—"

Suddenly they were all staring at Engineer's Mate Tom Ormsby.

"What?" I growled.

"Swimmin' would be amongst yere other accomplishments, laddie?" Charters asked.

I shifted uncomfortably in the murky waters near up to my knees. Hadn't any desire whatsoever to explore the rest of the Congo River's depths. "I'm a mere beginner, a—"

"Hah!"

They were onto me like vultures.

"That's more swimmin' skills than all the rest o' us wrapped up in one," Walker proclaimed. "Congratulations, laddie. Ye'll be the *Stanley*'s savin'!"

Hell's bones. Trapped.

Shortly I was being attached to a sling of ropes like one of my donkeys. My equally well-developed sense of self-preservation near set me into kicks and brays—but before I could disgrace myself, I was lowered over the steamboat's side with the first of the tin plates gripped in one hand.

The task was simple. All I had to do was feel along the *Stanley*'s hull for the holes just bored through it. Next, slap the plate over the damaged section of the hull and thread the strings attached to the tin through the holes. The engineers inside would snatch for the twine and shove a bolt through. Then all I had to do was screw on a nut. . . .

That's all I had to do. Submerged. In the Congo River. Bleeding agony. See if I freely offer my services for the next disaster that comes along. And there would be a next disaster. Sure as I lived and breathed.

How long I'd remain living and breathing was topmost in my mind as I slid into those murky waters.

"What about the crocs?" were my last words as the river began to swallow me.

"Never fear, old chap," floated down from Barttelot, safe and dry above. "I'll have my rifle trained on the buggers. I can pick them off wart by wart."

Wasn't the crocs' warts that concerned me. It was their teeth. I desperately filled my lungs—

Dark. Currents tugging. Something brushing my naked leg. Something slimy.

Get a grip. No sense in crying over spilled milk, Mum always said. You wanted Adventure. *Live with it.*

I groped for the hull. Ran my hand alongside it. Found the first hole. Slapped on the plate. Threaded the twine. Burst through the river's surface, gasping and heaving and kicking off the safety ropes that'd slowed me down.

"Did you find the holes?" Stanley peered down.

"First one," I choked out.

"Well done!"

I dove again. And again. And again.

For my reward, Stanley pulled me off my ship, stripping me of my column and friends.

"You're a useful sort of dogsbody, Ormsby. I think I'll keep you closer to hand."

Once aboard the *Peace*, Henry Morton Stanley forgot about me. He spent his days improving maps of the river. When we pulled into shore for firewood each afternoon, he'd haul out his aneroid and make atmospheric measurements. Wouldn't have minded learning more of the mysteries of the instrument, but he never invited me to join him.

Fortunately the *Peace*'s engine room was near in worse repair than the *Stanley*'s, and Mr. John Walker had no qualms about making me both welcome and useful. I spent a fair amount of time convincing the ancient works not to give up the ghost. When the temperature got too infernal, I went above deck. Wasn't much of an improvement. Africa still glided by, as darkly mysterious as ever. But hovering over the *Peace*, enveloping it, suffocating it, was the stench of rotting hippo. Jameson had bagged his emergency provisions back in Kinshasa right enough. Three two-ton hippopotamuses. The meat had been divided between ships, and the remainder of the *Peace*'s share was guarded by Soudanese and Zanzibaris alike with increasing anxiety. Their cook fires blotched the deck: pots filled with putridly green, maggoty hippo meat; the air above alive with flies.

Mercy.

Dead hippo. It sank into your very pores.

~~

Then came a diversion. We started steaming past villages again—tiny riverside collections of rectangular, thatch-roofed huts surrounded by palms and banana trees. Fair idyllic they looked, save for the fact they were empty huts, empty villages. Could tell these hadn't been ravaged, though. Dying cook fires still sent wisps of smoke into the air. I figured the terrified folks were cowering in the bush, praying for the passing of our belching boats.

The natives of the upper Congo kept themselves good and scarce till well into June. Then a few bolder warriors, smitten by curiosity, paddled a small flotilla of canoes close to the *Peace*'s hull. Come to learn we were in Basoko country—and these were the very kinsmen of Baruti!

Baruti. Stanley's silent shadow. Here he was, standing next to Stanley, only a few yards down the deck from me. Talking! Absolutely jabbering away to his master. Next, Stanley was hailing the canoes.

I moved closer. "What's happening, sir?"

"Amazing, Ormsby. Baruti has spotted his long-lost brother! I've invited them all aboard, but there's a natural reticence in these people. . . . Wait. The brother is asking something." He turned to Baruti.

"What does he say?"

Baruti cast down his eyes. "My brother does not believe. He says, 'Tell me some incident from before you were lost, that I might believe.'"

"Well, well," Stanley prodded, "go to!"

I watched Baruti squinch his eyes in concentration, then call out something. He gripped the railing the way I had back on the Thames. Whispered, "I say, 'Thou hast a scar on your arm—there on the right. Dost thou not remember the crocodile, brother?'"

A wild, jubilant whoop rang out. The Basoko slid his canoe alongside, grabbed for the railing, and bolted over it. He stood

for a moment in the glory of loincloth and bangles, then enfold-
ed Baruti in a great, joyous hug.

I backed away. The encounter was too private. The embrace
was too real. How long since I'd given a hug? Been hugged? Even
thought of a hug? Would I ever escape the inferno of engines and
rotting hippo to find my own family again?

The Basoko departed. Baruti stared after their canoes, trembling.
Stanley touched his arm.

"Do you want to go with them?"

Baruti swiped at his eyes. Shook his head no.

"Excellent!" boomed Stanley. "Too damn many Arab slavers
in the vicinity anyhow." He lit a celebratory cigar and puffed with
satisfaction as the last of the canoes skimmed 'round a bend in the
river, and even their ripples vanished. "Now might be the moment
to have another peek into the treasures of that Fortnum and
Mason's basket in my room, eh, boy? A good cheese? A little
pâté?"

Baruti shuffled off after the great explorer.

Two nights later, Baruti disappeared. He disappeared with
Stanley's personal Winchester rifle and a pair of Smith & Wesson
revolvers. Also missing were a silver road-watch-pedometer, a
little money, and one of the ship's canoes. And I never had gotten
a word out of him.

Just after dawn the next day we arrived at Yambuya, 1,100 miles
up the Congo at the confluence of the Aruwimi River. Stanley had
the steamboats stand offshore as he studied the collection of
cone-roofed villages through his field glasses. He passed them to
Jameson.

"What say you? Is this not the perfect spot for our supply
depot?"

Jameson focused on the hordes of Baburu natives gathering
on the bluffs fifty feet above the river. "The savages look restless.

What of them?"

Stanley shrugged. "If they cannot be bought, they can be frightened off." He nodded toward the interpreter already bobbing alongside in another of the ship's canoes. "Off with you, then!"

I hunkered over the railing to watch the negotiations. The first hour was spent in exchanging compliments. The second hour in coaxing a few residents down to the shore to accept a gift of beads and to learn what they'd accept as rent for their villages. The morning wore on, and the heat rose. The Baburu people expressed no interest in leasing their land. Stanley tired of shouting at the interpreter, tired of the game. He signaled for the *Stanley* to cross the river and join the *Peace*. Another signal from the master and both steamers let rip with their horns. The combined sound was more than shrill. It was deafening. The whistles screamed mercilessly on till even I covered my ears. When the last hiss of steam ricocheted between the riverbank and the forest walls, there wasn't a native in sight. Stanley thumped the railing with satisfaction.

"Advise the captain to approach the shore, Jameson. Disembark the men! Chap-chap!"

The mighty Relief of Emin Pasha Expedition scrambled up the steep bluff into the abandoned villages. And that's how we stole Yambuya.

Bloody Hell.

THE GREAT FOREST

THE GREAT FOREST IS WHAT STANLEY CALLED IT.
The rest of us? Anything from "Hell itself" to "worse than a fever
victim's wildest ravings." On June 28, 1887, we entered it. It was
a date I'd not soon forget. How could I? It was my seventeenth
birthday.

The reveille bugles roused me from a sweaty sleep.

"Rained all night again," I complained to my tent mate, Parke.
"More messy slogging."

He threw his legs over the side of his cot and rubbed his
watery, red-rimmed eyes. "At least you slept through it. I was up
half the night with Stairs. Where have you stashed that chlorodyne?"

"Dr. Collis Brown's finest?"

He grunted and staggered upright, reaching for his trousers
and boots. "The lieutenant's got a vile enteric fever."

"Intestines, eh? Bad business." I bent over a Burroughs &
Wellcome medicine chest, as scraped and weathered as the rest of

us, to root for a bottle. Stared at the level of its liquid, then counted the remaining bottles. "Getting low on supplies."

"More's the pity. Stairs is only the beginning. And the idiot refuses to be left here with Barttelot to recover. We'll have to carry him by hammock."

"Less fool, Stairs. After that scene last night, how'd you like to be left with Barttelot for the indefinite future?"

"Ah, yes." Parke grimaced. "As the brave commandant of Yambuya was ordered by Stanley to become blood brother to the local chieftain,"—a dry chuckle—"in hopes that our theft of land will be forgiven and a brisk trade for food will ensue."

The ceremony passed through my mind again. Especially the look of unutterable disgust on Barttelot's face when he had to lick a pinch of dirty salt from the flowing blood of the Baburu's slit arm. Then there was his other look as the chief cheerfully licked *Barttelot's* arm in turn, the one of sheer hatred aimed at Stanley. . . .

I shook off the scene and spread open the tent flap, taking in the camp. Stanley'd been busy in the last two weeks, for a cert. Hedging all his bets. After chasing off the Baburu people, Stanley had a secure wooden palisade built 'round Yambuya's former common land above the river's bluff, with a moatlike ditch circling its exterior walls. The outlying manioc fields were raided, and great sections of the forest gouged to fuel the steamers on their return trip to Leopoldville. All in the name of protecting and housing the rear guard of the Emin Pasha Expedition. *Bleeding misery.* Blood-brotherhood ceremony or no, there had to be a whole lot of unhappy natives hiding in that forest beyond. Bent on revenge.

I didn't have high hopes for morale within the palisade, either. Not with the choleric Major Barttelot in charge of Jameson and Bonny and a contingent of Zanzibaris and Soudanese. The lot of 'em were stuck here till Ward and Troup returned from Stanley Pool on the steamers—with the remainder of the expedition's supplies we'd left behind for want of space on the first Congo trip. In the meantime, the extra six hundred porters needed to transport the extra supplies to the advance column hopefully would also show up. The promise of procuring these porters is why we'd been lugging along Tippu-Tib. Why Stanley'd made his deal with the notorious slaver to begin with. I remembered watching the indolent rogue on the river cruise, relaxing under the gay awnings of the *Florida*. Tippu-Tib reclining upon pillows like a Caesar, slave boys fanning the air over his head . . . Tippu-Tib's whale-sized harem members revolving around him in a sluggish, heat-dazed dance as they vied to drop tidbits into his mouth. Brought on the shudders, that sight did.

"Barttelot's going to have his hands full," I conceded to Parke, as I tucked in my shirttails. "How'd you like the task of keeping diplomatic talks open with Tippu-Tib and his entourage without Bula Matari? Especially now that the lot of 'em have taken off for Tippu's stronghold in Stanley Falls?"

"Thankfully with the damned slaver's harem of fat wives," Doc croaked in answer.

I grinned. "Gone from whale-sized down to sow-sized the last we saw of 'em. And getting thinner every day." As were we all, with rations at an all-time low. When would our "great leader" learn to bargain for food with the tribes we trespassed upon *before* angering them?

I yanked my belt a notch tighter—

"Ta, Doc."

—And set off for my reconstituted column.

I'd thought sure Stanley was going to snatch me for his personal servant after Baruti decamped, but he'd picked Sali, a local village boy. Instead I'd been assigned to the advance guard of three hundred eighty of the fittest men, along with Parke, Nelson, Jephson, the ailing Stairs—and Henry Morton Stanley, of course.

An hour later, to the beat of drums and the porters' marching chants, we paraded through the palisade's gates. To one side was the Aruwimi River—on the other, an impenetrable wall of green. We plunged straight into it.

"Allah preserve us," Tewfik prayed behind me. "I like not this place."

The understatement of the century. I packed my rifle, cartridge pouch, and canteen as usual, but carried an unsheathed knife and kept my attention on the creeping canopy overhead. A thieving monkey swooping down was one thing, but the vipers and tree-dwelling green mambas Parke'd been telling me about were something else entire. One bite from those fangs and you were a goner. Only let venom *spat* by the wicked demons touch you, and you were dead meat.

"Halt!" rang out.

I near banged into the Soudanese guard at the tail end of Captain Nelson's column, but caught myself in the very nick. I halted hard, wiping the sudden sweat of fear from my face, then turned to Tewfik. "What happens, brother?"

He eased his load to the earth and wiped his own brow as he digested the Swahili coursing down the line like a telegraph message. "Godless savages not happy. Make many traps for us . . . hidden by grass in path. Pits. Stakes sharp like knives awaiting our naked feet. Poisoned stakes."

"The machete cutters up ahead are gathering the stakes? Making the way safe for us?"

"Even so." His eyes widened as he gave me a shove. "Down! Down!"

I'd long since stopped asking why. I ducked, then flattened myself as I saw a rain of arrows—undoubtedly poison arrows—piercing the tangled growth. I fear it took rather longer than it ought to have for me to clutch at my rifle, fumble for a cartridge, and send a shot into the beyond. The Soudanese guards got the idea and followed with a flurry of wild bangs. The rain of arrows stopped.

I lay there on the narrow footpath, breathing hard. Thinking maybe I should've taken more seriously the words of that wild witch Gulai back in Zanzibar. Should've taken the woman up on her offer of a personal talisman, the price no object. Too late. So I waited for the jungle sounds to return. The birds . . . the insects . . . Shut my eyes and thought about Mum. If I were home, she'd be happily cooking up a storm in the kitchen. Making all my favorite dishes. Bubble and Squeak. Toad in the Hole. Spotted Dick. Could almost hear Katie and Hannah squabbling over who got to lick the batter bowl, who found the most currants. . . . No, that was the howler monkeys. I opened my eyes with a sigh. Finally I crawled toward Tewfik. The urge was upon me to find a little human sympathy in the midst of all this madness.

"Today is the day of my birth," I confessed. "I would like to live through it. Would like to live through a whole new year."

Tewfik stopped searching his person for nonexistent arrows long enough to grasp my hand. "Today I pray for both of us, Bull Boy. *Inshallah*, we will survive."

God willing, indeed.

Nelson's porters began working forward again and I struggled up. Time to rally my men.

"What power have such puny arrows against our guns?" I bellowed. "Chap-chap! Get a move on!"

My Zanzibaris and I stumbled into our first jungle camp well after dark. I mumbled a prayer of thanks for the advance crew who'd put up the tents for the expedition staff; who'd even built a crude *boma*, or bush fence, around the rough clearing according to Stanley's specifications. Then I reeled through the flap of my home for the night. I'd barely yanked off my boots and collapsed on the cot when it began.

Nerve-shattering whoops.

Hair-raising howls.

Uuuuuuuuuuuuuuuuummmmmm—the long, low, eerie blast of tribal horns.

The jarring assault completely surrounded the tent, the

encampment. Making the night and jungle converge. Making even my mosquito net suffocating.

"Er . . . Doc?"

Parke sighed through the blackness separating us. "'Tis but flourishes and alarums. Take no heed, Tom. Only diversionary tactics to frighten us off."

I shivered in the thick, damp heat. Frighten us off to where? Back to England? Did such a place still exist? I meant to ask, but the sleep-starved Parke was already snoring, and to the steady metronome of the comforting rhythm, I slowly dozed off myself . . . . Till, much later I think, a new sound pierced the silence of the sleeping camp, startling me from uneasy dreams. Out of the forest came the voice of a deep-throated speaker . . . followed by an echoing chorus. I shook my head and tilted it to better hear.

"*Ho, strangers, where are you going?*"

"*. . . Where are you going?*"

A kind of play was being performed on the wildest of stages. Dark African theater. Perfect for the dead of night. Perfect for our camp's captive audience. The troupe presented a simple plot with simple words.

"*This country has no welcome for you.*"

"*. . . No welcome.*"

I rolled over to the canvas and peeked through a hole I'd been meaning to patch. The jungle was closer than it had any right to be, seemed already to be reclaiming the space we'd hacked from it, stolen from it. And floating through the void of blackness were pale, disembodied heads. . . .

"*All men will be against you.*"

"*. . . All men.*"

No. *Masks.* Grotesque, unspeakable masks with howling mouths and sightless, staring eyes . . .

"*Till you surely will be slain.*"

"*. . . Surely slain.*"

Horror blurred my vision.

"Ooh-ooh-ooh-ooh-ooooh."

" . . . Ooh-ooh-ooooh . . ."

I joined the unearthly moan as I buried my head in my arms. Many happy returns, Tom Ormsby.

Flaming misery.

My eighteenth year on this earth was like to be a trial. For a cert.

Fair restless, I rose before dawn to wander among my column. They sprawled in sleep like innocent babes under a waning moon. It soon became obvious that our night visitors had sent more than words through the darkness, across the "protective" *boma*—and the exhausted porters had slept through it all. Our sentries had, too. Spent arrows and spears harmlessly surrounded my Zanzibaris. All but one—

"Blast!"

I lunged for the spear spiking from Bhoke's body. He opened his eyes and blinked up at me.

"The sun does not yet rise, little brother. Give me some peace."

"Bhoke, Bhoke! You live! Thank God! Allah be praised!"

He stared at the ghostly spear I was wrestling from his mat, then at the gash its tip had made in his robes—less than an inch from his body. Sighed. "The Gardens of Eternity must await me another day."

I shook my head and strode off with the spear. This was the second time Bhoke had escaped death by a hairbreadth. How many chances did a man get?

The next few days we hacked through jungle and rambled into a dozen carefully concealed, freshly deserted villages. Stanley took his revenge on our nightly serenades of howls and threats by order-ing the expedition to descend on the abandoned manioc fields like a scourge of locusts. Unlike the hiding natives, the manioc fields fought back. Hungry porters gnawed the raw roots, then began clutching their stomachs in agony.

By the fourth day in the Great Forest, Stanley was forced to order an early halt. Parke shrugged impotently at the sight of sick porters strewn across the clearing—far too many sick to tend. "Will they never learn, Tom? The cassava root—genus *Manihot* of the spurge family—is mildly poisonous if not well prepared."

"Only mildly?" I asked, watching my men writhe in agony. There wasn't enough Dr. Collis Brown's Chlorodyne on the entire continent of Africa to cure their bellyaches.

"If eaten constantly in its raw state," he relentlessly continued, "the accumulated effects can become quite fatal."

I bit the bullet. Somebody had to. "How do you prepare it properly, Doc?"

Parke lit one of his precious few remaining cigars, considering. "From what I've gathered, you have your women pound the roots in the river, then boil them three times in different water, followed by grinding them into a kind of pulpy mush which is then re-cooked as a gruel—" He stopped to give me the eye. "Don't even consider it, Ormsby. These men will never lower themselves to do all that women's work."

I gave him the eye right back. "My men will." And off I marched to beard Tewfik at his campsite.

To give him credit, Tewfik listened. 'Course he'd reason to, curled up and clutching his own stomach like he was. After a pitiful moan, he said, "Too much work. A starving man cannot think so far. His eyes see food. He eats. That is all."

I snorted and spat with the aplomb of a Soudanese. "Our men will learn to think first." I flourished the *chicote* I'd unburied from my possessions. "By Heaven, I do not want to use this whip on any human being. Ever. But the first man of my column to eat another raw manioc root will be whipped till he chooses to think first!"

The surprise on my co-captain's face changed to respect. He

painfully wobbled to his feet. Swaying ever so slightly, Tewfik the Bold cleared his throat. He addressed his men.

"Hear this all! Our brother Bull Boy will save our bellies and our lives. You need only obey. You must obey or feel his whip!"

The general convulsions slowed. A few porters managed to prop themselves on their elbows. Others began thoughtfully brushing dirt from their robes while two fellows made a crawling dash for the nearest underbrush.

"We hear."

"Speak. What must we do?"

Tewfik methodically explained my culinary tips and their much desired result—the carrot—and concluded with the stick—a nod to my poised *chicote*.

"Pah, woman's work!"

"Huh. He'll never use the whip."

"Never!"

"Wherein lies this little master's merit? He is only a *mission boy*!"

My Swahili might be poor, but it was daily improving—a fact the men had forgotten. Being called a mission boy was the basest of insults, right down there with being compared to the illegitimate offspring of a dung beetle. Wasn't something I could let pass, was it? Not and keep face with my column. I flicked my *chicote* at the insolent fellow. Kept my wrist action good and steady but held back on the power, aiming for the equivalent of about a dozen wasp stings. "My word is good, Jojo. Take your slander back!"

"*Aie, aie, aie!*" Shocked disbelief filled his cry. Stomachache or no, he salaamed to me right sharpish. "A jest only, Bull Boy! A jest! I swear by the Prophet!"

I widened my stance and threw back my shoulders.

"I accept your apology."

In that pose I carefully studied the remainder of the men. Of a sudden they were quite alert. Amazing how the threat of new kinds of pain will take your mind off lesser ills.

"So. Your task is simple. Gather the remaining manioc. The stream awaits to cleanse it. Begin the pounding. Begin the building of fires for the boiling. By nightfall you will have a good meal prepared. There will be enough to fill your gourds for tomorrow's march and the next day's. Thus, Tewfik the Bold and Bull Boy's column will thrive. Thus, you will live to see Zanzibar again. You will live to watch your women prepare your roots while you lounge by the cooking fire."

A slow murmur rose from the men. It grew.

"*Nyanza, Nyanza*, cheer for Bull Boy!"

Me and my *chicote* stalked off. Such adulation fueled Henry Morton Stanley. All it left me with was a taste as bitter as raw manioc.

The Great Forest was endless. Steaming days. Enervating nights that ran into each other. On one of those nights I yanked off a boot and thumped it onto the canvas floor of the tent. Tugged off a sock and made the mistake of examining it too closely. Half-shod, I limped to the tent flap.

"Stop!" Parke exclaimed.

"I was just going to fetch a tub of water to soak my feet and wash my socks—"

"Not barefoot. Never barefoot!" My tent mate near gagged. "If you could have seen the tapeworm I pulled from the sole of an *askari's* foot just before supper! It measured nearly three yards. And they're picked up by bare feet in the larval stage."

"Thanks for sharing that, Doc."

Ever so carefully I leaned out and grabbed the waiting tubful of water. Hobbling back with it, I began my ablutions. More than three bloody weeks into the forest we were. Dank, misty mornings worse than any London fog; endless stream fordings submerged to the waist . . . Well, it'd given our bedtime preparations a certain necessary ritual. I began the ceremony by stripping off my patched trousers and settling on the edge of my cot to begin soaking my feet. Next I turned the trousers inside out to examine all the seams for hidden ticks and leeches. Meanwhile, Parke was lighting a cigar. A cigar? I inhaled its sweet aroma. Watched the cloud of hovering insects around us recoil.

"I thought you were out of tobacco two weeks past!"

"Too true. But I finally got Lieutenant Stairs on his feet today. Stanley was so pleased that he restocked my supply for the foreseeable future."

I shifted to hang the trousers from a hook on one of the tent's poles. Made it easier to shake the scorpions out in the morning. "Stanley's been hoarding?"

"What do you think? He's still got at least ten of those Fortnum & Mason's baskets under guard."

"While the rest of us—"

"Sup on cassava patties and green bananas."

I sighed. "Sometimes I almost wish Barttelot was around to bag a decent meal. Warthog would look prime about now."

"Wouldn't do a bit of good, old chap," the surgeon assured me. "With the mile-long procession we're dragging through the jungle, every bit of game in its right mind is long gone. Here, stand up a moment."

No questions, I just stood. Something near scorched my thigh—

"Hah! Got the little devil!"

Parke shoved the cigar back between his teeth and presented me with a bloated leech. "Nothing like a fine cigar to deal with leeches," he gloated. "A good head of ash and heat dissuades them remarkably." He savored another puff. "Ready for our evening cocktail, Ormsby?"

"Can hardly wait, Doc." I sloshed out of the water, paused to toss the sated leech outside our tent—a little more of my blood offered to the gods of the jungle—and reached into the open medicine chest. Selecting a full bottle of quinine, I handed it to him.

"Let's see now," he murmured, uncorking the bottle. "We've

been doing ten grains a day since Yambuya. Things being what they are, feverwise, I think I'll increase the dosage by another ten grains." He reached for our water jug and two tins cups. "Sorry, but Stanley's largesse did not extend to seltzer water."

I froze. "You mean to tell me he's got seltzer water?"

"You don't want to know what all the man's got, Tom. To paraphrase 'The Charge of the Light Brigade,' ours not to reason why—"

"—Ours but to do and die," I finished, then muttered, "as if bloody Alfred Lord Tennyson ever set foot on a battlefield or in a bleeding jungle."

"Do I detect a trace of bitterness?" Parke handed me my mug. "Forsooth. A waste of energy and emotion."

I went along with the next little piece of our ceremony. Clicked his cup, and as it was my turn, made tonight's toast. Always the same toast, it was, without fail: "To survival! Bottoms up!"

"Bottoms up!" T. H. Parke echoed.

We drained our quinine cocktails.

Twenty grains of quinine didn't do the trick. Doubling that dosage probably wouldn't have, either. When the fever picks your number, there's no escape. So far I'd been lucky. I'd been Bull Boy. Invincible. Could be that's why it came down on me as hard as it did.

It began innocently enough a few days later. I'd wandered up the line to learn what'd set off roars of laughter, a little comedy being hard to come by these days. Poor solemn Jephson had gone and fallen into an elephant pit. No elephants were present, more's the pity, but it did take a certain amount of ingenuity to pull him out unscathed. So there he was, hopping up and down like Alice's Rabbit, too short—Stanley's height in point of fact—to reach the porters' hands fluttering over the edge of the hole. And there was Stanley himself doing a little jig around the pit.

"A rope, by all that's holy! Have none of you the sense to send down a rope?"

My grin faded as a chill overtook me. I glanced up in search of the sun. *Don't be a silly bugger, Tom. Haven't seen the sun in days, have you?* Can't expect to, either, with all those miles of trees overhead, shielding the rays from us. Screening them out, but holding the moist air below so tight, the temperature down here was as hot as under the lid of one of Mum's boiling pots. . . . Mum. The girls. Hadn't thought of them in a long time. My teeth began chattering.

Blistering Hell. So why's it so cold of a sudden?

"Hurrah!"

I focused back on the elephant pit. Jephson'd caught the rope and was emerging in triumphant little yanks. Wasn't funny anymore. My chills and I returned to my column.

"Looks like the cold-dry phase, Tom," Doc declared as he felt my brow that evening. He threw a blanket over me as I shivered convulsively on my cot. I burrowed within it.

"That'd be the . . . be-beginning of the fever," I stuttered. My teeth refused to stop their infernal clacking.

"'Fraid so, old chap."

"How . . . how long's it last?"

Parke was mixing our evening cocktail. He brought over my cup and raised my head so I could sip. "I upped the ante. Another ten grains. Can't hurt. One never knows with the bark of the *cinchona* tree. Drink up now, sport."

I blocked the cup from my lips. "Are . . . aren't you forgetting something, D-Doc?"

He frowned, then his face lightened. "How could I?" He reached for his own cup and clicked mine. "To survival. Bottoms up!"

"B-bottoms up!"

What followed the cold-dry phase of malaria was the hot-dry phase.

Blistering agony.

It's burning up, I was. And my brain was fair minded to burst, pounding worse than the explosives Bula Matari'd set for his road to Stanley Pool. I became that road as hundreds of feet—thousands of porters' feet—trudged over my aching body. My skin came undone from their heavy treads. It peeled away, leaving me with a new skin . . . a new color . . . even a new head of hair.

"*Jambo,* Mum!" I cried, after scrabbling my way clear from the upper Congo and across the seas to that beloved red-brick London house. "Katie! Hannah! *Jambo!* Hello! Don't slam the door on me!"

"You'll never be our Tom," Mum declared. "I sent off a fair-haired lad. It's no wooly-headed, coal-black African I'll be takin' back in exchange!"

"*Tafadhali!*" I begged. "*Mbaya!*" Then, inconsequentially, "*Neno zito! Mtu mgumu! Maji machafu!*"

"Tom. Tom—"

I opened my eyes. Squinted for my lost London. Only a dank canvas tent. Only Surgeon T. H. Parke. I sighed. "Where am I, Doc?"

"In the jungle, where else?"

I reached to loosen my collar and found I was shirtless. Glanced down. Fair stark naked, for a fact. And still unbearably hot. 'Least most of my skin was still attached. I grappled for my head. No tight curls. Would it've been that bad? Turning native? No, it could've been interesting . . . aside from Mum and the girls. That London Missionary Society needed to start thinking about the natives as *people*, not just heathen souls only good for toting up points in Heaven.

Another sigh. "How long've I been out?"

"Seven days. Tewfik's men have been coddling you in a hammock like a babe. The situation even got amusing when I had to bring Tewfik into our tent to interpret for you last night."

Tried to shift up on my cot, but was too weak. "Water? Could drink up half the Congo, I'm that thirsty. The Aruwimi, too."

Parke brought me water, and I struggled onto an elbow to sip it.

"It's not the Aruwimi anymore. Now they're calling it the Ituri."

Another new word. It jostled my scattered brain. "What . . . what d'you mean about Tewfik interpreting?"

Parke laughed. "You were most impressively delusional—raving in Swahili! Your bosom brother was beyond amazed, but still couldn't make sense of your wanderings. How could he, with you spouting things like, "a serious matter," or "a hard-hearted person."

I considered. "Was that all?"

"Hardly. After 'please' and 'bad,' it seems 'unclean water' was foremost on your mind."

"*Tafadhali . . . Mbaya . . . maji machafu,*" I mumbled. I collapsed back onto the cot. "So what's the prognosis, Dr. Parke?"

"Halfway through the malaria attack, Tom. You're halfway there."

I fear I whimpered in a most un–Bull Boy way.

"You lack but the hot-wet phase."

"Bad?" I asked.

"Mostly uncomfortable, followed by a prolonged period of lethargy. You're almost home free, Tom. You're strong. You can do it. You need only keep exerting yourself, keep fighting."

I grinned up at him. "You're beginning to sound a lot like my mum, Doc."

I must've sweated off another twenty-odd pounds during Doc's "hot-wet" phase of the fever. Lucky there wasn't much in the way of mirrors on hand, 'cause I didn't need to see the skeleton that'd be leering back at me. Still, didn't matter, did it? Not much mattered. Parke's "period of lethargy" had set in.

I swayed through the jungle's perpetual twilight in my hammock.

Today it was wiry little Bhoke and flamboyant Jojo doing their turn at the poles. Seems the men had been fighting over the honor of bearing Bull Boy. I didn't give a fig. Just rocked through the greenery like some pampered maharaja, catching bits of gossip along the way.

—"Bula Matari, he puts walking boat together. Takes to river beyond rapids like a great captain!"

That'd be the big canoe *Advance*, built in sections of steel for this very eventuality. Good. Less weight for the men to carry.

—"Soudanese must row." Snickers of delight.

Nice to get some work out of the *askaris* after all this time.

—"Babu Parke hunts birds, shoots guinea fowl!"

Meat for dinner?

—"Eight men lost in jungle! Seventeen rifles gone!"

So. The real desertions had begun. I yawned and settled more comfortably into the curve of my hammock. Let the screeching cicadas lull me into another little snooze.

HUNGER ROAD

IF IT HADN'T BEEN FOR THE BATTLE, I MIGHT'VE been lethargic still.

The evidence that we were in danger of attack had been building, but I was an empty shell—limp, near emotionless. In my dullness I ignored the omens. It was hard to ignore entire villages scorched to the earth one step ahead of the Relief of Emin Pasha Expedition, though. Harder to ignore baby skulls littering the charred ruins or women so freshly dismembered that the vultures hadn't even got their fill of them yet.

Flaming torture.

I tried to shrug off the signs, the violence. I tried mightily.

Then something clicked in my brain. Like fitting together a puzzle on pleasant evenings back home. The girls would clap with delight when that last little piece of the jigsaw fell into place, showing a pretty scene of Paris, France. But the scene snapping into place here and now wasn't pretty.

"Bhoke. Dedan. Set me down. Please."

"But our place of stopping is just over the next hill, little brother," Bhoke protested as he shifted the weight of the poles on his bony shoulders. "We have strength to finish the distance."

"Now!" I ordered. "And bring me a rifle and cartridges."

They dropped the hammock with a thump. I crawled out and up. Tested my legs. Firmer than expected. Stretched a hand for the waiting rifle—in the very knick.

A volley of shots broke out ahead.

The startled porters backed away from me in awe.

"Bull Boy knew!"

"In his sickness, Allah has enlightened him!"

I strapped on the cartridge pouch and loaded the gun in record time. "Murdered women and children," I growled. "Butchery enough to enlighten me. Drop your loads and ready your guns! Chap-chap! There's trouble ahead!"

The next barrage of shots came from over the rise. Another volley led me through our deserted evening camp to a view overlooking the Ituri River. There were Lieutenant Stairs and some fifty of his men sheltering behind the steel hull of our beached boat. They were firing with relish at ranks of warriors lined up on the far shore of the river.

Seemingly endless ranks of men: wild of hair—with wilder scowls and howls—stamping to drumbeats even as they nocked their arrows to bowstrings. More ferocious native warriors than I'd ever seen, or hoped to see. We'd caught up with the savage pillagers at last.

I swung my head in search of my column. Nary a man had followed me. Probably cowering behind their packs. Not that I could blame 'em. Hadn't signed on as soldiers like the *askaris*, had they? Back I turned to the war zone, back to watching our bullets do little more than shatter trees and add frothing ripples to the river. Sheer enthusiasm couldn't hold a candle to proper marksmanship, could it? We were outnumbered and outpowered. And the Ituri was at a narrow point in its channel. The arrows of the warriors flew fast and free across its width. If the enemy was allowed access to its waiting canoes . . .

I hesitated on the very brink of it all. Not from fear of those arrows, poisoned though they surely were.

Bloody Hell. How could something so terrible be so beautiful?

The sheer deluge of brightly feathered shafts swarming through the air like a flock of jungle birds near mesmerized me. Time stopped as they hovered—then the deadly birds fell. Straight into our little army. Thomas Grenville Ormsby hadn't signed on as a soldier, either, but I knew in my gut the job was covered under "general dogsbody." Everything was. I readied myself to plunge down the hill.

Wait—

Stairs was rising above the boat's shelter. Gun pressed to his shoulder, he carefully picked a target, carefully pressed the trigger. As the bullet raced across the river to carefully strike his prey, an arrow thumped into the lieutenant's chest. I watched his graceful swan dive onto the sand.

Mercy.

Tiny skulls and body parts and the lieutenant's dance clouded my vision. Whooping as terrifyingly as the savages, I roared into battle.

"A very pretty set of villains. Look here."

Surrounded by his remaining officers after the fighting was over and done, Stanley examined one of the bodies that'd washed up on our side of the battlefield. "The brute's wearing a coronet worthy of a king." He eased off the golden headdress and added it to his pile of booty. Then he continued his analysis, as dryly as some Albert Hall lecturer. "Observe the iron drops set above the lips and drilled in patterns into the chest." He pried open the corpse's mouth. "The filed teeth." The jaw clacked shut. "And the necklace,"—he tugged it over the lolling head—"human teeth, unfiled. Ah yes, we're dealing with cannibals here. Avisibba warriors."

Jephson nervously chewed on his mustache. "Working on their own, sir?"

Stanley glanced up. "Not at all, not at all. They're obviously in league with the Manyuema—the tribe hand in fist with the savage leader Ugarrowwa."

"That'd be the slaver chap that Tippu-Tib warned us about," commented Nelson.

"The same. From the looks of the last few villages, he's collecting another string of slaves for Zanzibar. Clever devil. It also gives him free porterage for his hoards of ivory. A two-for-one return on his investment." Stanley bent again to the beach, this time retrieving a spent arrow. He studied its tip, but was smart enough not to touch it. "Still stained with poison. And the shaft . . . sorry, my dear fellows, but it would seem well-enough constructed to give our guns some competition in both distance and accuracy. As we've already noted from hard experience. Vexing."

I'd been squatting on the shore at the edge of the discussion. Catching my breath. Sorting my mind. Not sure I wanted to see the new picture that was forming. Wasn't every day I shot at least five human beings.

Bang-bang-bang-bang-bang.

Fast as I could reload and aim and pull the trigger. I'd gone somewhere far beyond those seagulls tailing the SS *Navarino*. Gone so far . . . I gulped another heaving lungful of the thick air laced with death. Worst of it was, I would've picked off another five if the cannibals hadn't packed it in. Just abandoned their canoes and melted back into the Great Forest. Would've picked off another ten—

"Ormsby? Give us a hand if you're able, will you?"

It was Surgeon T. H. Parke, crouching over one of the wounded porters. I joined him as Stanley began fondling an Avisibba bow. Didn't need to hear the rest of his lecture, did I? Already knew how strong the wood was. Already knew how powerful a weapon it could be. Already got my revenge for those women and children. So why didn't I feel justified, like one of Pastor Gribbins's Avenging Angels of the Lord?

Stairs had the exclusive use of his own hospital tent. The eight wounded Soudanese and Zanzibaris were jammed under a makeshift canvas of their own. Surgeon T. H. Parke and I spent a long night traveling between tents.

"Never worked with poison arrows before, Tom," Parke muttered as we hovered over Stairs. "Medical literature in England didn't cover the eventuality." He studied the arrow still protruding at a belligerent angle from the lieutenant's chest. "Awfully near the heart. But come out it must."

He looked up at me, seeking some kind of verification. Fair pitiful he was. Hadn't shaved in a few days. Hadn't trimmed his hair in a few months. Now its lankness fell across his damp spaniel eyes. He swatted it away.

"Absolutely, Doc. Just give it the old heave-ho!"

"He who hesitates . . ." He gripped the shaft. "Ready?"

"Count of three," I answered. "One . . . two . . . three—"

"Ungh!"

Parke yanked. Out came the gory arrow. Below us Stairs yipped and sank back into unconsciousness. I slapped on a quick dressing to staunch the flow of blood, then felt for his pulse.

"He's still with us, Doc."

T. H. Parke sighed. "Thank the Lord." A pause. "I'm awfully glad you finally knocked the fever, Tom. Welcome back."

I rocked on rapidly weakening legs. "Thanks. Thanks for pulling me through."

"Turnabout is fair play, eh? I still could be buried under that monster tree along the Congo. According to the Chinese, that would make us responsible for each other into eternity." He cleared his throat. "Right, then." Another swat at his hair. "Next we inject sterile—well, boiled river water, at the least—into the wound. Try to flush out the poisons. Tidy up the whole mess—"

"And pray," I concluded.

Besides the battle-wounded men, there was a sudden plague of festering ulcers among the carriers. Nasty they were, as if the jungle was trying to gnaw into the very marrow of their bones. This was on top of the usual tapeworms and the generally anemic state of near the entire expedition. All that said, Stanley made the decision to dig in for a few days at our current camp above the Ituri. About the only ailment of the lot that could be easily cured was the anemia—but that required food. So Stanley sent Jephson off into the forest with a column of the healthiest men. Their orders?

"Forage for anything it's possible to swallow!"

We were long past the tiny jungle clearings with cultivated manioc fields. Thinking back on them, those pitiful farming villages seemed the height of civilization compared to our current digs. That's how far gone we were. With even bananas and plantains at an all-time low, the remnants of the expedition listlessly sprawled around our river camp waiting for Jephson's return. No such rest for the doc and I. We were still trying to save Stairs. He seemed to be rallying, unlike the four porters we'd lost to the Avisibba's arrows.

"We gave them the same care, didn't we, Doc?" I asked, as they were lowered into shallow graves.

"I tried, Tom. By God, I tried. But when a poison arrow strikes home in a vein, all bets are up."

By the third day after Jephson had taken off into the forest, it became obvious that he'd gone and gotten himself lost. Stanley prowled around camp snarling at anyone in sight, then finally made a decision.

"Juma! Find your best trackers and send them after Bwana Jephson!"

The Soudanese snapped to attention. When his search party

disappeared into the dark clutches of the hovering jungle, we were left with only eighteen functioning men—and too many sick to count. A fine moment it was for the Avisibba to renew their attack. Nature beat the cannibals to it.

It began to rain just after dawn the next morning. Wasn't any old soft and misty forest shower, either. More like the steady 330 shots per minute fired from the Maxim automatic gun Lieutenant Stairs had played with way back in Matadi. Been lugging the monstrosity ever since, but our officers hadn't yet managed to set it up in time to be useful. Anyhow, it was that kind of downpour, along with an entire week of monsoon thunderstorms, all packed into sixteen hours.

The sick sought shelter under plantain leaves or Avisibba shields or just slung copper cooking pots over their heads and whimpered at each new jagged onslaught of lightning, each new boom and crash of thunder, each new painful inch of driving rain. I felt like whimpering myself.

Suffering torment. Need to escape. Nowhere to escape to.

I set off under my own makeshift umbrella of leaves to the ridge above the Ituri. Stood there soaked to the bone, overlooking the battlefield. Listening to the river growl. Watching it grow. Watching the water's color swirl into a milky brown . . . like a huge cup of tea with milk. All that tea was churning down the Ituri to pour into the Congo, to pour into the Atlantic. A wrench of longing near overtook me. Would the ocean currents carry this Ituri tea north to England? Would I ever again sit in our cozy little London kitchen with a cup of Mum's tea?

"Ormsby! There you are!"

I spun. "Doc?" Then he accomplished the impossible. He pulled laughter from me. Wonder of wonders, Surgeon T. H. Parke was sheltering under a bed pan!

"Enough of your ruddy insolence! Necessity is the mother of invention." He shifted the pan to a jauntier angle and grinned. "Been hunting all over for you. You've never seen a proper case of tetanus, have you?"

"The very thing to brighten my day!"

"Come along. We'll be awarding you a medical degree before this adventure is up."

Parke wasn't joking. With pleurisy and dysentery cropping up on top of everything else, I was getting plenty of what he called clinical experience. Kept me too busy to turn mawkish again, too.

Meanwhile, we'd given up on Jephson's return anytime soon.

"The young idiot can just follow our tracks! And Juma, too!" Stanley declared as we continued the march two days after the Great Rain. Mid-afternoon the healthy porters got wind of a handful of abandoned chickens. Chaos took over the line. Down their packs toppled. Off they bolted, rifles in hand. They banged at those poor creatures like they were the Avisibba, with the self-same results. They scared the dickens out of the poor chickens for a cert, but never bagged a single one. All they managed to accomplish was shooting one of the Zanzibaris in the foot. It was Tewfik who helped carry the man back to me. There my co-captain stood, eyes downcast, blood splattered all over his robe, hanging on to the poor writhing sod's leg.

"Tewfik." I sighed. "You, too?"

"My eyes overruled my head, brother. Once more."

Wasn't any point in losing my temper, was there? The damage had been done. "An empty stomach has a way of overruling all," I said.

He lifted his eyes. "Allah protect you, my brother. Your wisdom grows like a young prophet."

I swallowed my snort. "In Allah's name, Tewfik, carry Egarrowwa to Babu Parke before he bleeds to death upon you."

Messed up the Zanzibari's foot right proper, that shot did. Parke had to amputate it just above the ankle . . . with me assisting—and eight of the victim's friends holding him down. The experience left me wondering whether medicine was meant to be my life's work. It truly did.

Juma and his trackers caught up with us six days later. Without Jephson. The errant officer himself crawled into camp two days after that, shamefaced, as well he might be. Put everybody to a lot of trouble, hadn't he? To add insult to injury, he'd lost four men. Not to mention that his food-finding mission was a complete disaster. *Blazes.* Can you really count rats and beetles and slugs as food possible to swallow? That night I poked at my share on the tin plate before me. No amount of re-heating was going to make it palatable. Parke had fewer scruples. He tore directly into his rations.

"Yum. Certain nutlike quality to the beetles, Tom. Nice crunch, too."

I gagged, then stoked up my courage for a nibble of roasted rat. 'Least it was certifiable meat, wasn't it? Chewed. Considered. Swallowed. "Smoky. On the tough side, though."

"Even rats get old."

"In the jungle? Then we can live in hope. I thought sure nothing survived here that long!"

Parke snorted and attacked another beetle.

There matters stood till the last day of August, when Juma the Soudanese ran off with fifty pounds of biscuit.

"Fifty pounds of biscuit!" I yelped when Doc passed on the news during our usual private supper in our tent. "Why weren't *we* eating that biscuit!"

"Before it could be absconded with?" Parke calmly asked, as he had a go at a plateful of fried ants.

Big buggers, they were. With wings. Maybe closer to termites? In sheer desperation the porters had lopped off the top of one of those ten-foot mounds that erupted like misshapen monuments all over the place. Staring at my plateful, the memory of those Giant Madagascar Hissing Cockroaches in Zanzibar's bazaar grew fonder by the moment. Doc broke into my reverie.

"Want to put the question to Stanley? About the biscuit?"

"Probably saving it for bloody Emin Pasha," I fumed. "Though how Emin Pasha could be in worse shape than his relief expedition beats me—"

"**Emin Pasha**!" A sentry's cry rang through the camp. "Emin Pasha! He comes!"

"Emin Pasha? Here?" The tin plate and its disgusting contents slipped from my lap. Just as quickly, words I'd never meant to voice to another human being slipped from my tongue. "That means we don't have to spend another three hellish months getting to the end of this miserable, godforsaken jungle! We can hand over what's left of the Emin's bleeding ammunition. Let *him* kill the next round of cannibals!"

"Let *him* keep his ill-gotten ivory," Parke gleefully joined in.

"We can head for home!" I whooped. "Certain sure we're bound to run into Barttelot on the way back, and he's got to have all the missing supplies by this time, and there's bound to be *some* food mixed in the lot—"

Doc crowed. "And we can fatten up everyone!"

Laughing hysterically, we stomped on our fallen clumps of winged ants in a wild victory dance, then tripped over each other getting through the tent's flap. And there was Stanley dashing from his own tent, madly jamming his arms into his ceremonial coat. The one with all those gold-braided frogs and epaulets.

"Where was he sighted?" Stanley roared.

"On river, Master!" the sentry cried. "Big canoe! Very big! Red flag flies on it. With crescent moon. Same like ours!"

"Egyptian standards?" Henry Morton Stanley took off at a trot for the river.

Every able-bodied man in camp raced after him.

And there was the canoe. It was big, right enough, and it was flying the Egyptian flag—but it turned out to be carrying nine—

"Manyuema tribesmen!" Stanley exclaimed. Then he hailed them.

"Who is your master?"

"The Arab Uledi Balyuz, known as Ugarrowwa," the bowman answered.

"Where is he?"

"Eight marches upriver."

"Tell him the Relief of Emin Pasha Expedition comes to call upon him."

"The way will be made open. A feast will be prepared!"

The Manyuema dug in their paddles.

As they disappeared upriver, Stanley began ripping open the frogged buttons of his ceremonial jacket. His face had gone red. His shaggy eyebrows lowered threateningly over smoldering eyes. Of one mind, the expedition opened a path for him as he strode back to camp.

"An evil day," he raged. "An evil day. Now we have that damned slaver from Hell and his pet cannibals to contend with."

A long sigh of despair spread through the crowd. I turned to Parke. "No Emin Pasha. Think we can scrape up our ant rations?"

Our way was prepared, for a cert. The gates of the first village we encountered the next day were decorated with the freshly hacked pieces of a little boy. About Hannah's age, he would've been. I lurched forward to further empty my empty stomach, narrowly avoiding the speared woman lying just inside the gates; catching the complete eerie emptiness of the rest of the village—aside from the selection of fly-covered grinning heads decorating the tops of half a dozen posts. The volcano in my innards kept erupting, but there was nothing left to spew forth. Stumbling on wobbly legs, I cursed Stanley rather than the Manyuema. Stanley who was serenely cruising in tandem with us on the *Advance*. Stanley who would calmly shake off this outrage because he'd never personally laid eyes on it.

While this latest horror was being digested by the expedition at large, five carriers made off with four loads of ammunition and a load of salt.

Having pretty much reached the bottom, truly the depths of despond, wasn't anywhere to go but up, was there? Henry Morton Stanley in his infinite wisdom pulled us back into life. Not intentionally, of course. The man hadn't an ounce of humor in him. Thank the Lord, most of the rest of us did. Guess I'd have to thank the Lord for the elephant, too.

A great rogue bull, he was, with tremendous tusks. The very next day he came storming out of the jungle, out of nowhere, near flattening Tewfik and me.

"Tewfik!" I gasped, as I sprawled in the dust of the track. "Was he real?"

My friend raised himself on an elbow. "Only look. He has opened a path to the river. To make such a path would take ten men with machetes and billhooks half the day! Only listen. He rips another tree from his way!"

With the next crash from below, the very earth trembled beneath me. I scampered up. "It's my first elephant, Tewfik. My first true, wild elephant. *Alive.* Who could believe they're so huge, so powerful, so . . . "

Running out of words, I made for the new path to the river. Hanging on to a tree trunk, I looked down. There was the bull, having a fine splash in the river. And there was—

"No!"

"What happens?" asked the dozen porters suddenly scrambling behind me.

"Stanley comes in his boat! He sees the elephant! He . . . he raises his gun!"

"His five seventy-seven bore?"

I squinted. "Yes. His biggest gun."

"Ho. Meat tonight!"

"Meat . . . meat . . . meat!" the porters chanted.

Even as my stomach grumbled with hollowness, I protested. "But not this elephant. Not this magnificent elephant!"

Stanley fired. The boom reverberated through the river's gorge. My elephant stopped frolicking to plunge his trunk into the river. As the second shot sounded, he raised his trunk—and attacked Stanley and his rowers with a titanic blast of water! The porters began to chuckle as they pressed closer.

"The Great One fights well!"

"A worthy opponent!"

Another shot, another blast of water. And so it went, until Stanley stopped to examine his weapon.

"The Great One destroys the gun!"

"See the Master's anger!"

"Even Bula Matari cannot break this one's spirit!"

"Ho, no meat tonight."

And then, inexplicably, the porters began to laugh. I laughed, too. What could be more wonderful than an elephant taking on civilization's mightiest sporting weapon, taking on the world's mightiest explorer—and winning? I was still laughing when the bull trumpeted triumphantly and turned around.

"Whoa! He's coming back up!"

"Allah protect us!"

My men raced for their lives, and I along with them. But long after the mighty rogue bull rammed his way back into the jungle, the grins stayed plastered to our faces. Even better, my column broke into its long-abandoned marching chant, and the rhythms took us cheerfully to our night camp.

Wish I could say otherwise, but our elephant diversion didn't stop the desertions. Not with the threat of the slaver Ugarrowwa looming ahead. When nine more men scarpered off, Stanley called a general muster. What was his solution? He ordered the rifle mainsprings removed from every carrier's gun! Now they'd lost their value, making desertion useless. Maybe it never occurred to Stanley that worthless weapons couldn't fight Ugarrowwa's cannibals, either.

Blistering Hell. What next?

Next was the camp of Ugarrowwa himself. Our land columns

neared it a few afternoons later, paralleling Stanley's riverboat. Suddenly wild gunshots cut the air! Gripping my rifle, I turned to Tewfik behind me. His eyes were wide with fear.

"I cannot help you, brother. My gun does not work."

"You may raise your prayers to Allah instead."

Just ahead was a point with a clear view of the river. I called a halt. Readied my single rifle. Before it was steadied against my shoulder—

Singing! The beat of drums! Bursting out of nowhere!

The festive music intensified as it wafted downstream, closer and closer. I lowered my rifle as Tewfik dashed up beside me.

"What happens?" He stared. Smiled. "Allah has listened."

Floating into view was a flotilla of canoes. Enthroned in the largest—surrounded fore and aft by the fattest women and the healthiest men I'd laid eyes on in what seemed like forever—was Ugarrowwa, robed and gilded in the wilderness like some pagan king. To the jangle of song, drums, ululations, and muskets popping off like fireworks, the slaver paused mid-river for a chat with Stanley. Tewfik and I watched as food, *real food* was loaded into the *Advance* from his canoes.

"Goats," Tewfik whispered. "Rice. Plantains. Chickens."

"Hurrah!" I roared, as we near pounded each other senseless. "Tonight we eat!"

THE SLAVERS' WORLD

WILLINGLY OR NOT, WE ENTERED THE SLAVERS' world. That night we set up our tents across the river from Ugarrowwa's fortress. I near had to haul out my *chicote* again to keep my men from attacking our portion of the food stone-cold raw. But soon I, too, was gorging on tough hunks of goat seared black on the outside and bloody French rare inside. Even caught Jephson griping about a bowl of rice he called "a little too *al dente.*" Didn't keep him from scarfing it down, either. And after every scrap of food was gone, there was singing and dancing to the beat of drums around the columns' campfires. I lay on my cot listening and smiling. It had been too long.

In the morning I woke to a sight that took me straight back to Zanzibar. Our camp had been turned into a bazaar! The slavers' people had crossed the Ituri in canoes to barter food for ammunition, beads, near anything—and business was brisk. I rubbed my eyes, then set off to bargain what I could for my own stomach.

The fun ended with Stanley's return from an official visit with Ugarrowwa. One glance at the chief's canoes, and he saw red. He chased them off for fear of losing more ammunition to barter, then turned 'round and raved about the slaver to our camp.

"The man's got himself a mud palace with public rooms commodious enough for an audience with Victoria herself! And treasures! The tons of splendid ivory . . . "

The *this*, the *that*, the *other*. I cautiously tucked into my sack the feathers of the plump hen I'd acquired for a mere handful of cartridges. Stanley kept going on like he hadn't the least idea what Ugarrowwa's business really was. Like he hadn't heard about those skulls and hacked bodies the rest of us had seen while he was cruising in his bloody boat. When I couldn't stand any more, I interrupted.

"What's the man after, then, Mr. Stanley? Why did he give us food last night?"

Stanley frowned at me. "It was a gift. A gesture of diplomacy from the master of these parts to Bula Matari." A little strut before returning to earth. "His supply of gunpowder is also nearly exhausted, and the villain is looking to us for more."

Another glower, and Bula Matari continued tallying Ugarrowwa's wonders.

"He also had the prettiest little dwarf lady, from Pygmy tribes farther inland. No more than thirty inches tall, with the eyes of a young gazelle, and a glossy, sleek, perfectly mature body . . . "

The prettiest little dwarf lady *slave*! I wanted to scream. Still and all, I had eaten the slaver's food last night . . . and mightily wished I could've seen that Pygmy lady. Torn between guilt and desire, I slunk off to hide my booty of hen and potatoes and manioc flour, then to help Parke prepare our sickest patients to be ferried across the river. Slaver from Hell or no, Ugarrowwa'd made a deal with Stanley. In exchange for three hundred pounds of gunpowder, he'd look after the ailing porters until we could return for them. The thought of being fattened up on all that compound's food near tempted *me* to play sick. I wasn't the only one harboring such mutinous thoughts, either.

Two mornings later I tallied up my column before beginning another long day's march. Several familiar faces were notably absent. I searched for Tewfik at the front of the line.

"*Jambo*, brother," I saluted him. "Where is Jojo? And Bhoke?"

Tewfik the Bold's face crumpled down to his chin beard. "Dedan say they hear game. Go in search of it—"

"With their full packs of ammunition . . . and rifles?" Functioning rifles, I didn't bother adding. Stanley had seen the error of his ways with our full entry into the slaver's territory, and re-issued the missing parts.

Tewfik shrugged.

What was the point of dressing him down for not controlling his men? The point of anything? "Enough stalling!" I bellowed. "Chap-chap! Let's get moving!"

The next night's camp was scarcely set up when an ominous rustle shattered the quiet of the jungle lying in wait around us. A prowling beast, suitable for supper? Past hoping for that miracle. The return of the cannibals? I grabbed for my gun, aimed it at the spot—

And out of its blackness came Jojo, and Bhoke, and a third man—Ali, of Nelson's column. They staggered into the clearing near bare. Oh, they were wearing their robes, right enough—a little more soiled, a little more tattered—but that's all. Gone were their ammunition packs and rifles, while right on their tails, prodding them forward, were a half-dozen well-armed— *Remington*-armed—Manyuema. Stanley swept forward.

"What is the meaning of this?"

"A gift from Ugarrowwa," was his answer.

The Manyuema and our usurped rifles flowed back into the jungle's dark embrace. Stanley turned his attention to the three

99

deserters. I could see his color rise, his shaggy brows lower in threat. Fair obvious it was the man'd reached the end of his tether on the subject of desertion. He clapped his hands.

"Convene my court!"

Tewfik and the other Zanzibari captains stolidly assembled. In silence they gathered their robes and squatted in a ring around him. Stanley lowered himself in the center of the circle. A long pregnant moment passed before he addressed the men.

"Greetings, my children. I have a question that troubles me greatly. Perhaps your advice could help to answer it." Another pause to make certain he had the "court's" full attention. He proceeded. "Are not our rifles and ammunition our only means of defense?"

Solemn nods.

"If a native steals them, would we not shoot him?"

More nods.

"Well, then," Stanley continued with a gesture at the three prisoners Captain Nelson was guarding beyond the circle. "What are these doing but taking away our means of defense? If you have no rifles left, or ammunition, can you march either forward or backward?"

Mutters of, "No, Master."

"Just so." Stanley clapped his hands again. "You have condemned these thieves to death."

I sucked in my breath.

Bhoke, Bhoke. Two escapes from death were not enough? Still you press your luck with Allah's mercy? And brash Jojo. My men, both of them. My column's first desertions.

Bloody Hell and bleeding misery.

Stanley wasn't through. Far from it.

"One shall die tonight," he intoned. "Another tomorrow. Another the next day." He glowered at the gathered expedition members. "From this day forward, every thief and deserter who leaves his duties and imperils his comrades' lives shall die." To top it all off, Stanley made a washing-of-his-hands motion, just like Pontius Pilate. Finally, he rose. "Let them cast lots for tonight's execution."

The rest of the court rose after Stanley. Then Tewfik touched my arm.

"Do you have paper, my brother? For the lots?"

"Tewfik, I—" No more words came from my choking throat. No more were possible. I went to my tent and threw open my trunk. The first paper I laid eyes on was bound in a book— my Bible. It had aged since its presentation: mold had disfigured its leather binding; insects had gorged on its pages. The jungle was ecumenical in its destruction. I ripped out three pages at random. They seemed fitting for the purpose. Hadn't a Christian just condemned three men to death?

I presented the pages to Tewfik. He jerkily trimmed two of the sheets to half and quarter size, rolled them up, then stumbled forward to offer the lots to the prisoners. I watched them choose: Jojo with his usual dash; Bhoke with resignation; the third—Ali—with eyes already dead.

My friend bent painfully to study the results . . . while the tension mounted.

Tewfik stiffened his spine. "Ali has chosen the short lot," he proclaimed to the waiting crowd. To Ali, "May Allah forgive you. May He take your hand and walk with you."

After that, it all went fast. Nelson heaved a rope over a stout tree branch. Forty of his men laid hold of the rope as the prepared noose was thrown over Ali's head and tightened around his neck.

"Have you anything to say for yourself, Ali of Zanzibar?" Nelson barked. Always the proper officer he was, doing up the affair by proper English rules.

Ali shook his head.

"Pull!" Nelson ordered.

I turned to the jungle as the porter was hoisted up. The jungle. It ate into more than arms and legs and books. Now it was gnawing at our very minds and souls.

~

The dangling man swayed over the too-silent camp. There were none of the usual jokes. None of the endless complaints. And sure as Hell itself, no singing. Only the quavering "good Lord deliver us" lament of nightjars filled the darkness. My mind was made up. It had been for the hour I'd paced the tight quarters of the tent. Just took that long to build up my courage. I pulled my boots back on and headed for the flap. Parke glanced up from writing in his diary. Raised an eyebrow.

"Stanley. I'm going to see Stanley. He can't continue this madness!"

"Can't he?"

I stormed out, but I wasn't the first. I strode directly into a delegation of the Zanzibari captains. Tewfik was at its head, Rashid of Nelson's column beside him.

"Tewfik." I reached for his arm. He was quaking beneath his robe.

"Leave me, my brother," he begged. "I must face Bula Matari on my own legs."

I'd forgotten. Jojo and Bhoke were his men first. "Tonight," I whispered in his ear, "you truly earn your name of *Bold*."

As I eased into the shadows, Stanley flung open his tent flap. There he stood, haloed by the lamplight like some fallen saint. He addressed the captains for the second time that night.

"Nothing can be gained by talk when the crying stomach rules. An indelible impression must be made on the rest of the men. An indelible lesson. The die is cast."

Tewfik threw himself to the ground and salaamed. "Good Master, your lesson hangs over this camp still. Few will sleep for thoughts of the morning and the next morning. Cannot another way be found? Another lesson that will leave the remaining prisoners . . . alive, to repent?"

Stanley made a great show of considering this request. Smoothed his hair. Tugged his shirt cuffs. In the end, he invited the men into his tent for further discussions. I crept back to my own.

Come dawn, Bhoke pulled the short lot. Under Stanley's supervision, Captain Nelson chose another tree for the execution. Ali still dangled from the first, didn't he? And the topmost limbs of its neighbors were festooned with hulking vultures. Patient as death, they were. I spat out of principle. Knew they were only doing their job, but I hated them, anyway. Hated thinking of those carrion eaters finishing off Ali, finishing off Bhoke. I turned from the vultures in time to catch Nelson throw the noose round Bhoke's neck. He tightened it precisely, then about-faced to ready his forty hangmen.

"Wait!" Rashid cried.

He and his brother captains rushed toward Stanley and flung themselves at his feet.

"Forgiveness, Master!"

"In the holy name of Allah—"

"Have mercy!"

Stanley pulled at his neatly trimmed mustache and humphed a few times while the entreaties grew into wails that sent shivers up my spine. The master yanked at his spotless jacket. At last Henry Morton Stanley lifted his arms in forgiveness.

"Enough, children! Take your man; his life is yours. The last prisoner's as well. *But see to it.* In the future there is only one law for him who robs us of a rifle—death by the cord!"

Caps and turbans flew into the air. Hundreds of fists punched toward the open bit of bluing sky over the camp. Hoarsely complaining vultures abandoned their roosts to circle above.

"Death to him who leaves Bula Matari!"

"Show the way! We will follow!"

I backed off, watching Stanley bask in the scene he'd orchestrated, watching him *grow* within it. Backed right into Parke. He steadied me, then pulled at his cigar and sent a cloud of smoke to join the celebration.

"Never underestimate our noble leader, Tom."

"I wouldn't think of it, Doc."

I stalked off toward the forgotten Bhoke. Somebody had to remove his noose.

Famine followed euphoria. We marched for days between wind-falls of plantains and nothing. Stanley staunchly voyaged on in the *Advance* till the cataracts of the Ituri River grew so overwhelming that even the stubbornness of Bula Matari couldn't conquer them. Then he picked a desolate site atop the cliffs. Strewn with boulders, it was, and hemmed in by impenetrable jungle on one side— and a sheer drop to the Ituri on the other. There he left the *Advance* in sections. He also abandoned the now-ailing Nelson and fifty-two of the sickest men, not to mention the loads of ammunition they wouldn't be carrying. What he didn't leave was food. Wasn't any, was there?

"The termination of the jungle—the plains, verdant with food—lies no more than two weeks ahead," Stanley addressed the forsaken. "Be of good cheer! You will be relieved at the earliest opportunity."

Stanley lived in a perpetual tunnel. The man couldn't see aught but the light of Emin Pasha at its end. Like Mum's china bulldog come to life, he was. Had his jaws locked on the conclusion of the affair, and nothing was going to distract him enough to loosen 'em. Promptly casting one of his best officers and the sick porters from his mind, Stanley marched the rest of us from the camp as the endless thunder of the cataracts crashed six hundred feet below. I reached for my neck, damp like everything else from the rising mists. The sheer starkness of the place, the moaning waters, it all tightened around my throat like a noose.

"Starvation," Tewfik muttered behind me. "There is nothing here for the body but to starve. The spirit, also, in such a place. Allah protect those we leave in this *Starvation Camp*."

Once past his lips, the name stuck.

Two weeks to the plains? *Bloody impossible.* We'd left the ribbon of river which had given us a margin of safety from the jungle. 'Least that's how I saw it. Now we were completely swallowed by the Great Forest's uplands. It put me in mind of Jonah in the whale. Everything breathed around you. In and out . . . in and out . . . sucking the very oxygen from your lungs. Dark as the innards of a whale, too. Twilight it was. Permanent twilight even at full noon. The sun never managed to fight through Parke's bleeding flora. So why'd the stuff seem to grow new tendrils before my very eyes? I yanked the creeping abominations from my face with each new step, too weary to worry about dangling snakes. Saw one of those vipers now, I'd have it in a stew pot before it even thought to bite me.

On we bumbled through virgin paths hacked by our machetes and billhooks. We blindly followed Stanley and his quest, foraging as we went.

The second night inside the belly of the whale, Parke took it upon himself to give me lessons. Turning from the desk he'd stacked together from our near-empty medicine chests, he raised a cautionary finger.

"Have a care for the wild fruits and berries out there, Tom."

I slumped on my cot. Dripped from every pore of my body. Ached in every bone and joint. Heaved for air, breathable air. "Where'd you get the energy to start up on a lecture, Doc?"

He was stripped down to his drawers same as me. Sweating as bad, too. Even the ends of his drooping mustache dripped. Yet he grinned. "The principle of a stitch in time. A revelation granted to me during our lovely afternoon stroll."

I managed a snort.

"Ah, you may well ask. What was my brilliant insight? A simple one, but true: the expedition's only two medical men need to remain physically functioning—within the parameters of the jungle, of course."

"Some bleeding parameters," I griped.

He wagged his finger. "Nonetheless. Pay attention. No matter how delectable they look, only go for fruit you can see the birds have been after. They've had generations of experience evading the poisonous varieties. As for the fungi,"—he opened one of his books—"look here. Come and study these illustrations."

I forced myself upright to squint over his shoulder in the dim lamplight. "They all look the same to me."

"Not at all, not at all! Here,"—he planted his fingertip on the border of an etched plate—"is your standard edible European forest mushroom, of the class *Basidiomycetes*. Note the thin stem and its flattened cap, its dull brown and gray colors, while here,"—he turned the page—"this little beauty . . ."

I stared at the red-tinted mushroom with its cap seemingly bigger than a parasol.

"One bite of that," he enthused, "and you're deader than a doornail."

I sighed. "What I wouldn't give for a simple plowman's lunch at the pub down the street from work—"

"Babu Parke! Babu Parke! Come quick!"

We spun toward our open flap. It was Sali, Stanley's servant boy.

"Master eat forest pear! Eat many! Master dying!"

"Could that mean the Fortnum & Mason's baskets have been emptied of their last tin of pâté? Their last cheese?" I asked.

"Cynicism ill becomes you, Ormsby. You want to be stuck in this hellhole *without* Stanley?"

Pausing only to shove his bare feet into boots, Parke grabbed for his medical kit and ran. I followed for the clinical experience— at my own pace, thinking about the doc's last question. The Relief of Emin Pasha Expedition without Henry Morton Stanley? *Hell's bones.* The very idea of losing our leader, pretensions of grandeur or no, chilled me despite the oppressive heat. He was the only one who had an inkling of where we were going. He was the only one—whether he cared or not—who could get me, Tom Ormsby, out of the disaster I'd volunteered for. Out of the Congo and home again. The man was irreplaceable.

I found myself whispering a prayer as the surgeon emptied our writhing leader's stomach. When I bent to wipe Stanley's feverish face with a damp cloth, and he opened his eyes and growled at me, I said another prayer. This one in thanks. I also decided then and there to dodge the jungle's wild fruits and fungi entire. Grubs and slugs and caterpillars were safer.

Two weeks past Starvation Camp we stumbled into Ipoto, one of the fearful Manyuema's ivory camps. Since boldly marching from Yambuya at the confluence of the Congo and the Aruwimi with a strength of 386, we'd left 58 men in Ugarrowwa's care. We'd abandoned Nelson and another 52 at the top of those wretched cataracts. Along the way, another 104 men had either deserted or died of starvation, battle wounds, drowning, or hanging. Our fine advance column of the Relief of Emin Pasha Expedition now counted no more than 171 members. Ipoto looked like salvation to each and every one of us.

Come to find, this lot of Manyuema was in league with Kilonga-Longa, Ugarrowwa's top competitor for slaves and ivory in the upper Congo. Also come to find that between the two they'd divided and laid waste to hundreds of thousands of square miles of the Great Forest.

"How d'you picture hundreds of thousands of square miles?" I asked Parke before bedding down that first night in Ipoto.

"France," he answered. "It's the same size as the Great Forest. You picture *la belle France* covered with jungle and swarming with cannibals."

I drifted into restless dreams of the Cathedral of Notre Dame of Paris pictured on my sisters' jigsaw puzzle. The glorious church came in and out of focus while being devoured by a relentlessly marching, ever-growing jungle. . . . Cannibal drums and rank upon rank of wildly feathered arrows announced a savage attack on the survivors seeking sanctuary in Notre Dame's towers. . . . More drums. I opened my eyes.

Bum bum bum-ba-bum bum bum.

No dream this. The rhythm throbbed through the canvas of my tent.

Bum bum-ba, bum bum-ba, bum bum-ba—

The tempo was increasing, taking on a frantic edge. Having long since repaired the spy hole in my tent wall, more's the pity, I struggled from my mosquito net and crawled to the flap. Parted it just enough to catch the glow of a great bonfire in the open square beyond. Ghostly dancers were swaying around the fire. Their naked bodies were slathered with white clay from head to toe. As the drums and the dancing rose to a mad, frenzied crescendo, another dancer leaped from the shadows into the circle. His body was painted, too, but this one was different. He was in charge.

He wore a vast furry cape of animal skin over layers of amulets; a topknot of a bigger, fiercer monkey head than I'd ever imagined—and a mask. He stamped round the rising flames to the pulse of the drumbeats, brandishing a wickedly lethal blade in one hand. Turned . . . let out a bloodcurdling screech . . . and stopped cold to face me head-on. The drums pounded around him, the ritual continued, but he remained frozen, crouched like a beast on bulging legs, knife stiff, ready for the plunge.

Into me.

By all that was unholy, this witch doctor sensed me. Saw me. Saw right into me. Was trying to skewer my very soul.

Bleeding agony.

Couldn't will my eyes away. His pull was stronger than claw-faced Gulai's. A thousand times more powerful. The mask. A different kind of horror from the pale, wailing faces of my first Great Forest night this mask was: round as a full moon, a black moon; inlaid with brass and gold that flared in the firelight; a gaping mouth that *screamed*—

With a superhuman effort I broke contact. Scrambled back to my cot and flung an arm over my eyes. Didn't help. Didn't wipe out the mask's image, its infernal summons. The drumbeats and the screaming face tortured me till morning.

Wasn't any big surprise about Ipoto and its new lot of slavers, but now we knew for sure why we hadn't passed any happy villages with thriving plantain and manioc plantations. Knew for a cert we'd not find any more beyond Ipoto, either. The Arab chiefs had a simple operating plan: kill all the men who refused to be shackled; capture the women for slaves or harems; capture the children to be raised as new raiders; hack up anybody putting on a fuss— and eat 'em if you got the urge. Polish it all off by torching to the ground everything that was left.

Didn't stop any of us from gorging on Kilonga-Longa's food. Didn't make any of us protest the piles of ivory littering the compound, not to mention the scores of newly enslaved natives. Was I the only one silently fighting my conscience? The only one with nightmares? Was I the only one who'd heard the drums? Seen the dancers? Been skewered by that mask? I daren't ask. Daren't verify it was real, not just another one of my regular night terrors.

Come morning, the expedition was one big bellyache. One big headache, too, from the palm wine that'd circulated with the food. Couldn't move, could we? Could barely think.

Stanley negotiated a deal for us to stay and recuperate for nine days.

The gifts of food stopped after two meals. Beyond that it was every man for himself. Three thousand rounds of ammunition and too many rifles disappeared in short order. Stanley hanged a man and flogged twenty for selling cartridges. The Manyuema joined the fun by spearing Jojo to death for allegedly stealing corn from their compound's fields. Tewfik and I had hardly buried and begun to mourn the rash, but always so alive Jojo, when the savages awarded two hundred knife cuts to another porter, using the same excuse of theft.

On the ninth day, Stanley finally convinced the station's Manyuema—by dint of offering blood brotherhood and rich gifts of cloth and bangles to its chief, Ismaili—to loan the expedition thirty healthy slaves to carry supplies for the long overdue relief of Starvation Camp. Jephson, Parke—and I—were ordered to collect Nelson.

STARVATION CAMP

IT WAS A RELIEF TO ESCAPE THE EXPEDITION.
A relief to get a little distance from Stanley and even my own
dwindling column. It was also a relief to march with healthy
porters again. But the biggest relief was the incredible feeling of
well-being a fellow got from having unlimited access to the food—
also begged from Ismaili—those porters carried.

"Do I see a spring in your step, Tom?"

Parke caught up with me as I was playing leader on the
second morning out from Ipoto. I'd actually begun to enjoy
the jungle around me. How all those creeping vines had managed
to grow another dozen yards in our few days' absence. How they
were festooned with orchidlike blooms I'd never noticed. How
iridescent green-and-purple seed-eaters and the most extravagant
parrots swooped through the low insect hum ahead of me.

"Could be, Doc. It's sheer amazing how easy the trek is with a
full stomach and the way already cleared. Also amazing being at
the front of the caravan for once."

"Like Stanley." He chuckled. "Enjoy the view while it lasts, old chap. Enjoy the fleeting authority, too. I think I see Jephson heading this way."

"Bloody Hell." So much for my sense of power. I deflated fast.

"I say, it's not as bad as all that." Doc patted my shoulder. "There's no way Jephson can get us lost on this trip."

"No, but he can annoy us to death."

Even then I heard the crack of his whip and the nervous, high-pitched tenor of his "Chap-chap! Chap-chap! No time to lose!" closing in on us.

I took another deep breath of jungle air. Amazing how you could smell perfume through the decay when a hundred sets of bare, shuffling feet hadn't churned the road ahead of you to dust.

"The devil with Jephson." I strode jauntily forward, practicing a fair imitation of those squawking parrots and the *poop, poop, poop* of the curved-beak hoopoe nonchalantly crossing my path.

It was also amazing how fast we made our return to Starvation Camp. Mid-morning of the third day, I heard the falling water. My high spirits dissolved into the mists beginning to rise around me. That crawly sensation took over—only this time it was worse, much worse. Every hair on my body bristled.

Blazes. Wasn't gonna be any picnic waiting for us at the top of this cliff.

We'd abandoned Nelson and fifty-two Zanzibaris. Nelson and five Zanzibaris were who we found at the top of that cliff—but two of those five were such skeletons it was clear they'd never make it through the day.

Jephson went into hysterics. Parke grabbed for his doctor's kit. Nelson sagged against a boulder, legs splayed uselessly before him, tears streaming down his emaciated face. I turned to the stunned porters behind me.

"You," I pointed to the first. "Drop your load and make a fire." To the second, "You. Find some cook pots." To the third, "Fill them with water." I gestured at the caged chickens on the head of the fourth. "Wring their necks!" Still they gaped like stone statues at the piles of rotting bodies littering the camp.

"Chap-chap! Do I need to find my *chicote?*"

It was the fastest pot of soup I ever hope to make. The fastest pot of gruel. I eased the broth down Nelson's throat first, then the throats of the remaining Zanzibaris. By the time I'd begun moving the gruel around, Nelson started talking.

"You left me on the sixth of October. . . . On the ninth I sent off Uledi and thirteen of the best men I could find in one of our emergency canoes . . . to find food. They got lost." He struggled upright against his rocky chair.

"Take it easy, old boy," Parke said, homing in with his stethoscope again. "The telling will wait until you're stronger."

"Here, now." I swatted away the instrument and got in a spoonful of gruel.

Nelson took forever mouthing it, like his teeth'd gone loose on him. They probably had. Scurvy wasn't the only toll of starvation, either. He'd turned into an old man. His face was all tight, lined skin. And his hair—well, it'd been getting fair thin on top in the course of the journey, but now. . . . He caught my look and weakly raised a hand to his head. What was left fell out in clumps. I shoved another spoonful of gruel between his lips to distract him. His hand fluttered down, and eventually he swallowed.

"On the tenth . . . eleven men stole the last canoe . . . and deserted."

Blast it all. The army hadn't been starved out of him yet. The man had to follow regulations. Had to make his full report, didn't he?

"On the fourteenth, the first man died . . . on the fifteenth, the second. . . ."

Captain R. H. Nelson, late of Methuen's Horse, continued his relentless tally of desertion and death all the way up to the here and now.

"On the twenty-ninth of October 1887, . . . relief arrived."

Duty done, he closed his eyes and sagged away from his granite support. Parke caught him. "Get a proper tent set up, Tom. One for the other poor sods, too. We can't be moving any of them today."

"Will do, Doc." I shoved off my knees and grabbed for the bowl of gruel.

"Wait." He caught me. "One more thing."

"Yes?"

He nodded toward Jephson who was mooning around the clearing, still dazed. "Give that one a sock that'll flatten him— before he takes himself over the cliff."

I grinned. "My pleasure, Doc."

Come morning, it was a pretty fair bet that Nelson and the last three of his men would survive their ordeal under Surgeon Parke's continued care. This being the case, I was given an escort of four porters and sent in advance of the relief group with messages for Stanley. I safely stashed the letters in my cartridge pouch and studied the misty clearing a final time.

Like ghostly wraiths, Kilonga-Longa's remaining porter-slaves labored in a slow moaning dance. They were on burial duty. They were burying the dead. They were also burying the seventy-pound packs of ammunition that had been so carefully weighed at sea aboard the *Madura*; that had been so painfully carried up the Congo to Stanley Pool; that had cruised 1,100 miles by steamboat to Yambuya; that had broken countless good men in the Great Forest—till being dumped on this cliff above the cataracts of the Ituri. The ammunition would remain buried here with its dead guardians forever . . . unless many more porters could be found to rescue and carry it to Stanley.

Bleeding agony. The sheer folly of it all.

I turned from Starvation Camp and never looked back.

Made the return to Ipoto in record time, but Stanley was long gone. He'd left another lot of starving Zanzibaris behind at the mercy of the Manyuema. I studied the men slouched in the compound's dust, halfheartedly slinging pebbles at the ever-encroaching troops of monkeys and baboons. Found familiar faces.

"Tewfik! Bhoke! Dedan!"

We embraced as if it had been a year and not a week since parting. I disentangled myself for a closer look at my friends. Tewfik's bare head read like a map, a river of skin invading his short graying bush of hair. His little beard was newly salted with white. All three were stripped down to loincloths. "Where are your robes? Your turbans?"

Tewfik shrugged miserably. It was hard to hang on to one's pride and position without the robes—tattered though they might be—of civilization. "These miserable dogs of slavers. The Master is gone but an hour and the promised food is forbidden us."

Dedan spat. "May their skins be roasted in Hell. May they be renewed to roast again eternally!"

Bhoke only hugged his very spare jutting ribs and sighed. "What was left for us to barter, little brother?"

I clapped at the four porters behind me. "Many thanks for your help. You may leave your packs. Your work for me is finished."

I grinned at their retreating backs, at the parcels, then at my old friends. "Have you the heart to leave this abomination of slavers and journey on with me in search of Stanley?"

Their cries of joy were answer enough.

"Then let us see what we can find of use among the Emin Pasha's goods."

Those forty loads of fancy provisions from Fortnum & Mason's had rankled me long enough. So had the porterage of tons of ammunition for the Emin Pasha, who in my mind'd become nothing more than a colonial symbol for the status of an impossibly distant Britain . . . even worse, a symbol for the suffering of his relief expedition.

Bloody Hell. Past time it was for me and my friends to strike back.

We fell with glee on the loads I'd chosen with care and had carried from Starvation Camp: new robes meant for those now dead, leftover food. We trimmed down my tent to a piece of canvas large enough to protect the four of us in a storm. Then we stared at the last pack, full of ammunition. Finally, I clappedmy hands at the crowd we'd gathered.

"I would speak with Kilonga-Longa's station chief of Ipoto. I would speak with Ismaili. Chap-chap!"

The Manyuema rogue presented himself in his own good time, strutting in bright cloth and bangles. I squared myself before him, looked him straight in the eye, equal to equal, and took the offensive. Had to've learned a few things from Stanley by this time, right?

"Are you not he who made blood brotherhood with Bula Matari?"

Ismaili shoved his plump arm in my face. "You see the wound. It heals still."

I frowned. "And even as it heals, you dishonor your brother's wishes." I pointed around the compound, picking out the remaining groups of listless Zanzibaris still sprawled between huts and stacks of ivory. "Where is the food promised to Bula Matari's people?"

He grunted. "It is eaten. Their stomachs are bottomless, impossible to fill."

I nodded at the ammunition. "Would this help to fill them?"

Greed swam in Ismaili's piggy eyes. He lunged for the pack. "Continue your journey, Bwana Ormsby. All will be attended to!"

"No." I shoved his arms away. "You will bring me food for my hungry people. We will bargain. Cartridge by cartridge."

When my friends and I slipped back into the jungle from Ipoto, we traveled light, but we left behind more than a week's worth of food in the hands of the recuperating Zanzibaris.

"What kind of place is this, brother?" whispered Tewfik.

I shook my head. We'd been following the rough trail gouged through the forest by Stanley and his Manyuema guides. *Silently* following. Guess I'd had my own little revelation as front man for the relief of Starvation Camp. Huddling together under our square of canvas that first night out from Ipoto, I tried to explain it. "Have you ever heard the jungle breathe, my brothers?"

Dedan gripped his ears against the latest clap of thunder. "I hear it *howl*. Is that not sufficient?"

"It is not. Even the jungle breathes and talks. If we listen quietly . . . if we respect it . . . it can tell us many things." I paused for a bolt of lightning from the jungle's nightly fireworks to pass. Waited for the definitive *crack* as it struck entirely too close. "It can bring the animals back to us. The game our long, noisy caravan chased away."

Bhoke stopped trembling. "Meat."

I nodded as another bolt flashed from the heavens. "Meat to strengthen us."

Tewfik shifted at last. "We are only four. Our loads are not heavy. It is possible to set our feet down lightly—"

"To become one with the Great Forest," I continued. "To disappear into it, so our passing harms nothing."

Bhoke actually smiled. "Nothing but the game. When the meat will come to us."

"Allah knows, we are too weak for chanting as we march. Silence will be welcome." Dedan returned to clutching his ears.

So it was agreed. We would walk the forest with reverence, that it might open for us. Today, fresh from the night's storms, it spread into glades of colossal trees—forty, fifty feet around—that pierced the Great Forest's canopy at last.

What kind of place *was* this?

Like Tewfik, I was in awe of it. I was in awe of that single shaft of sunlight beaming down on the mossy ground around a behemoth. It put me in mind of the stained glass windows at Westminster Abbey, put me in mind of the cathedral's vaulting arches. How to explain that to a Muslim? But Dedan and Bhoke suddenly stiffened, and I hadn't the need to explain.

Blinding miracles.

Walking toward us through the aisles of the glade was a *Pygmy.*

I dropped the rifle from my shoulder, threw out my empty arms, and stared. He was a warrior, all thirty-odd proud inches of him. Had to be. His bow was nocked, and his arrow aimed straight for my heart as he came on fearlessly. Then he stopped . . . whistled a little birdlike flurry of sound. On impulse, I imitated the sound. Arms still outstretched, I repeated it, sending the strain ricocheting through the forest, from trunk to trunk.

I near laughed watching the fellow's face. Amazement. Wonder. Shock. More to the point, he lowered his bow. In a moment, the glade was swarming with Pygmies. And all I could think was, *faeries. Faeries do exist!*

That's all I had the chance to think, 'cause in another instant all four of us were surrounded. The men carried lowered bows, the women hunting nets—right along with babies slung on their backs. One group of women made a motion as if to throw their net over us. My man—the chief?—held them off while he tossed out a spate of words in that lilting, birdlike pattern. I listened for my life . . . heard phrases I recognized . . . bits of Swahili! Remembered the word for *friend*, and threw a swooping rendition of it through the forest. My man slapped his sides, snapped his fingers, and began roaring with laughter. In moments the entire tribe was hanging on to each other, near tears, then rolling on the ground with mirth. Tewfik poked me.

"What is this magic you make?" he hissed.

"No magic. Ventriloquism!" I slapped my own sides and joined in on the general hilarity. Never underestimate the usefulness of skills to be learned from *The Young Englishman.*

Bhoke edged next to me. "This is good?" he quavered.

I caught my breath and laughed with fresh joy. "I think this is good."

It was. The chief picked himself up, dusted himself off, reached up for my hand, and led me off. Just as nice as that. Like our dad used to do when I was a lad. I went as trustingly. Behind me, their loads crushing their turbans, Tewfik, Bhoke, and Dedan towered over the bevy of women leading them. Bhoke looked scared. Dedan's face was lit with a broad, snaggle-toothed grin. Tewfik had gathered his robe and was trying to look as bold as possible. And so we proceeded.

Beyond the cathedral glade, the jungle thickened again. We followed a narrow, almost invisible trail. At times even the Pygmies had to stoop to crawl through parts of it. As for me, I bumbled on, surely growing larger and larger by the yard. Some half-mile along, we came to a hidden village. I halted square in its center, stretching my cramped muscles. Looked around. Everything was neat and organized. But everything was *half-size*.

Mercy. Made me feel like Jack-in-the-Beanstalk's giant.

Luckily, huge heart-shaped leaves were spread on the ground. After much Pygmy miming and giggling, it became fair obvious these were meant to be our seats of honor. I picked a leaf and lowered my length upon it with as much aplomb as I could muster.

Much better. Near made me half-size . . . Anyhow, I got my wish to see a real Pygmy in spades, didn't I? Naught to do now but relax.

I sighed with pleasure and looked some more. Studied the dollhouse-like domed huts. Winked at naked children peeking shyly from behind their bare-breasted mums. Caught preparations beginning for what could only be a feast. I'd just begun wondering what'd happened to the chief when he popped out of the largest hut and strutted in my direction, twirling a kind of walking stick. He fiddled with the gadget, and it sprang into a little three-legged stool. After carefully arranging his tail-like loincloth, he enthroned himself before me.

The conversation began.

It continued in fits and starts while cook fires sprang up around us. Names were first on the agenda. Kenge—for so he pronounced himself—disdained *Tom* and didn't think much of *Bull*

Boy, either. Kept shaking his head till he lit up, slapping his sides in glee. That's when I was named all over again, this time after a tall straight sapling, the *fito*. 'Least that's what Kenge called it when he pointed out a sample growing on the border of the village. I nodded. Could live with that. Then the man went and tacked on the unpronounceable name of some noisy bird flitting around the clearing. A tall sapling was one thing, *Tall Sapling Who Sings Like Noisy Bird* was something else entire. I held up a hand before the business went any further.

"Whoa, now."

Stabbed at my chest.

"*Fito*. That'll do just fine, Chief."

"Fito." He clapped his hands with delight.

And so it went. Miming. Hand waving. Long clips and short bursts of talk. Along the way I began getting a better feel for the Swahili the Pygmies had adapted from the caravans plowing through their forest territory.

By feast's end, we'd dined on what I suspected was monkey, but decided it was wiser not to confirm. Didn't go down too bad with a sweet root called *itaba*. I'd maybe drunk a little too much of the homemade brew they called *liko*. Must have, 'cause it took me a while to notice that those shy Pygmy youngsters weren't hiding behind their mums anymore. They were crawling all over me worse than Katie and Hannah—yanking at my funny hair, poking at the curious color of my skin. Didn't give a fig. Kenge and I were great friends. All was well with the world.

Through my pleasant haze, it seemed like all was well with Kenge's world, too—with the entire Pygmy forest world, the *Ndura*. But of a sudden, the leader's face turned ferocious.

"*Kilonga-Longa*." He spat. Next, "*Manyuema*."

He beat his chest. Barked an order. Before I could blink, Kenge was poking a handful of arrows in my face; pointing out the poison-stained tips.

Sobered me up fast, those arrows did.

Bleeding misery. Kenge's people lived in fear of those marauding slavers, too. Only they were smarter than the bigger, captured natives. The Pygmies fought back. These people weren't any childlike innocents. Weren't faeries, neither. Just folks trying to survive. Same as me.

As thunder rolled in with the falling night, Kenge spread his arms in invitation. My Zanzibaris and I were to stay as honored guests. I squinted past the fire's brightness.

More miracles.

While I'd been head-to-head with Kenge, his people had gone and built another hut of slim *fito* branches and overlapped leaves. Twice as tall as their own, it was. Plenty big enough to hold the white giant and his robed comrades. I bowed to Kenge.

"Such kindness fair breaks my heart."

On another impulse, I bent over and hugged the little man. He hugged right back.

The Pygmy tribe wouldn't hear of us leaving in the mists of morning, either. When I crawled out of the hut and stretched back to full size, there was Kenge waving his bow, like he'd been waiting hours for my appearance. Probably had. His men were gathered, too, waving their own bows. It was a "You hunt with us" command. I turned to consult with my emerging Zanzibaris.

Tewfik spread his arms. "It is in Allah's hands."

Dedan was more forthcoming. "*Inshallah*, we catch elephant. My hunger is still great enough to eat entire elephant!"

We caught instead a *sondu*, an antelope—the first I'd seen of the lovely fleet creatures. And it was another wonder watching these little people accomplish what the great Stanley and all his guns could not. Had this hunting business down to a system, they did. The men set off in different directions with their bows and arrows. A bird call signified a sighting, whereupon half the tribe converged on the spot, hooting, chanting, beating the earth with sticks . . . chasing the cornered animal till it was half-mad with frenzy—straight toward the waiting women. The women closed in with their nets and cast them. *Pouf.* The antelope was captured. The arrows could do their work.

The return to camp was worlds different from the morning's silent departure. Songs and chatter filled the forest. Children danced round my Zanzibari friends as they proudly transported the game home.

Another night. Before the thunder surrounded us again, there was the celebratory music of the *banja.* Kenge sat and digested his food next to me, tapping his thighs in time to the rhythm of the sticks against hollow logs, watching his hunters dance an antelope dance. They performed it in masks, but these were *different* masks entire from my nightmares. Playful they were, like the Pygmies themselves. The carved and paint-daubed antelope heads sported wildly spiraling horns; their muzzles smiled benignly. The creatures bobbed and snorted and ran willingly into mimed nets. The dancers without masks snapped and roared, then bowed in thanks to their captives. Grilled *sondu* steaks were beyond good. The after-dinner entertainment beat that of any London music hall. I bowed my own thanks to the sacrificed animal and performers alike.

"*Asante,*" I repeated in Swahili.

Kenge beamed. Then he began a complex mime mixed with quick chatter. I watched. Listened to the new words I'd learned during the day. The meaning dawned on me.

"Blood brother. You want me to be your blood brother!"

I sank back abruptly. How many times had I seen Stanley become a blood brother? His arms were scarred with knife marks. But Stanley only accepted the honor out of political necessity. Here was I being invited out of *affection.* I launched a barrage of joyous whoops 'round the camp that stopped the hollow drum taps, stopped the whimsical notes of reed flutes. Kenge slapped his sides. Amid happy laughter, I bared my arm.

"No!" Kenge cried. "No Fito-Kenge. Fito-*Ndura*."

Fito-Ndura? He wanted me, Tom Ormsby, to be a part of his entire world? That was an honor way beyond blood brotherhood. Mercy. If a slash on the arm wouldn't do it, what would?

Kenge clapped once. The stick music began again, more intensely. He clapped a second time. "Moke!"

One of his tribesmen sprang forward with a ragged-edged arrowhead. One look at the ingrained dirt—and poison?—gave me second thoughts. Too late.

"Njobo!"

Njobo trotted up and caught me in a head lock. Like a vise, it was. I swallowed my protests manfully. Moke grinned and enthusiastically went at my forehead with the "knife." Felt like a slit in the center of my brow . . . then one over each eye . . . *Suffering torture.* Now Moke was gouging flesh from each fresh cut! I bit my tongue, tensed my entire body against the searing pain. Should've paid more attention to the scars on Kenge's face, the scars on his huntsmen's faces. But most Africans we'd come across gloried in such decorations. Should've figured out by this time they were more important than a scratched arm—

"Cephu!" Kenge ordered. "*Dawa!*"

Dawa. Medicine. Maybe there was hope. I was still in Njobo's fierce grip. I managed, though, to squint cross-eyed through the firelight at the little bowl Cephu was carrying. Some kind of evil-looking black paste inside . . .

Cephu dipped his fingers in the ashy mess and ground the "medicine" into my wounds with vigor. My body jolted of its own accord.

Yipes. That smarted some.

Then he ground in more. I tried to blink blood and ashes from my eyes. Just when I thought it'd go on forever, the grinding, the blood . . . Njobo released his grip. I raised my head.

Swiped at the blood. Waited for the dizziness to pass. Kenge presented me with a bowl filled with *liko*. I downed it in a gulp, then let the shudders work through my frame. The Pygmy initiation was done.

Hulking beyond the drummers, Tewfik shook his head mournfully.

Blistering Hell. You really went and did it this time, Tom Ormsby. Ever get out of this Congo and back to London, Mum will slam the door in your face. For a cert.

In the morning, Kenge and his tribe presented us with their greatest delicacy, wrapped leaves filled with honeycomb, then guided us back to the Great Glade. Couldn't see them, but I knew my Pygmy friends shadowed us all the way to the Balessé village of Ibwiri, where we found Stanley. For once the angels were on my side.

THE PEACEFUL FORT

A FELLOW'D HAVE TO BE BLIND TO MISS THE expedition's headquarters in Ibwiri. Only Henry Morton Stanley would have the gall to stake out his tent in the exact center of the sprawling village's communal square. I shrugged a shoulder at Tewfik, then abandoned my travel-weary comrades to present myself to Stanley. Cleared my throat—

"Thomas Ormsby, sir. Bearing messages from Starvation Camp."

"Enter."

Stanley turned from his desk and accepted the letters. His eyes rested a moment on my scarified brow.

"Going native on us, are you, Ormsby?"

"Just taking lessons from the master, sir."

His shaggy gray eyebrows twitched slightly. "That will be all."

No thanks for my messenger service. No interest in what really happened at Starvation Camp. No interest in when Parke and the others would catch up. No request for a report on his maligned porters at Ipoto. And, sure as certain, no interest in my trek from Kilonga-Longa's ivory station to Ibwiri. I about-faced.

"One moment, Ormsby."

I froze in place. "Sir?"

"Have a care for Ibwiri's fleas. It is the worst infestation I have ever encountered."

"Sir. Thank you, sir."

For a cert, Ibwiri had fleas. Still, I spent the following days of recuperation worried more about Stanley's sanity than the vermin population. I also tracked down the remaining medical chests and reinstated them in my old tent. With Parke gone, they made the place feel less empty. Next, I opened one and liberally anointed my Pygmy scars with alcohol and salve. But I was still too scared to look full in a mirror—even Doc's grainy shaving mirror, which I'd also reinstated with his other things. Finally, I considered the chests again. Wasn't much else to do while waiting for Doc and the others to turn up, was there?

"Tewfik!" I yelled out the tent opening.

He poked his head through the flap. "You call, brother?"

I waved for him to enter. He stalled.

What was going on? It finally hit me. Ibwiri's "civilization" had affected my friend. We were back to those bleeding class distinctions again. "Merciful Allah! Come in! Have we not shared shelter these many nights?"

"But not my brother's *private* home," he protested.

I scratched my head. Bloody fleas. "In Heaven's name, I have no patience for social differences. A man by any name proves his worth by his actions. Past time you learned that."

With the old salute to forehead, lips, and heart, he finally entered. I gave him a moment to take in the cots and mosquito nets, then got down to business, pointing at the medicine chests. "I'm setting up a clinic and would like you to be my new medical assistant. Morning hours only. You must spread the word."

He stiffened. I hadn't seen fear sweat beading Tewfik the

Bold's dark face for some time. At last, he shuffled uncomfortably before me.

"Surely Allah will reward you, my brother, but I am unworthy to be His vessel of mercy . . . unworthy to be yours. . . ."

Despite everything my Zanzibari companion had suffered and overcome, he was frightened of doctoring!

"Stuff and nonsense. A little puss and gore never hurt anyone. We've got to get our people in better shape for things to come."

His complexion went from mahogany to milk chocolate. His chin beard quivered. "Maybe Bhoke . . . no, Dedan! Dedan would suit the honor! He will prove a much better man than me!"

"No one is a better man than you, Tewfik!" I sighed. Had to give it up, didn't I? But saving face was everything. I reached for his shoulder. "Healing may not be an easy job for every man. This does not lessen his manhood. Fetch Dedan for me, please."

He salaamed. "Allah increases your wisdom daily, my brother!" Then Tewfik scampered off as fast as I'd ever seen him move.

I ran my clinic with the cheerful Dedan. In truth, his only failing was begging to preserve the tapeworms we extracted—inch by painful inch—by wrapping their heads around a stick of wood and winding till their tails appeared at last. I suspect he had a betting pool going for the longest specimen. His fellows would wager their hard-earned food on anything.

Jephson finally turned up from Starvation Camp the afternoon of November 16—alone. Seems he'd dumped the *Advance* in Ipoto. He'd also dumped Nelson there, for further recuperation, and Parke with him. I cringed at the news. Parke was too much of a straight arrow—and Nelson too ill—to have thought of digging up some of the camp's buried ammunition for trade. *Blistering hell.* Here we sat awash in food, and they were looking at more starvation under Ismaili's thumb. Stanley'd never give me permission to trek back to Ipoto to rescue them. He'd washed Nelson from his mind again. This time, Parke, too. And to add insult to injury, Stanley treated Jephson like a bloody conquering hero.

Life is not just.

We all waited some more. For Parke and Nelson. For Barttelot and Jameson and the rest of our rear column and supplies to catch up at last. No one was complaining, because Ibwiri was relatively safe, sitting as it did across some mysterious border from Kilonga-Longa's domain. More to the point, Ibwiri's Chief Boryo and his Balessé tribesmen were willing to accept us in their midst, were willing to barter reasonably for food. Yet we were closing in fast on a full year of this horrendous expedition, and I for one had had enough. Up to my Pygmy scars and more. Its end couldn't come fast enough. The men started filling out again, till they started chafing at the bit, too. When we finally decamped from Ibwiri the morning of November 24, our sole surviving Soudanese trumpeter blew the call to march with a gusto that was sheer amazing.

"Ready, aye ready, Master!" the columns roared.

Like old times it was. Almost. If you ignored the fact that we left Ibwiri with barely one hundred recovering wraiths, Stairs miraculously healed from his arrow wound, Stanley, Jephson, and me. I mourned for Parke still back in Ipoto. Even missed Nelson a little. Wasn't aught to do about it, was there? I turned to my short column.

"We march out of the Great Forest at last. Chap-chap!"

The strange thing is, we really *did* march out of the Great Forest at last. On the fourth of December, it was. Like my birthday when we'd entered it, it was a hard day to forget. The canopy suddenly broke into a clearing—a clearing that went on for *miles*. As the Zanzibaris dashed past me to fling themselves on the open earth in prayers of thanksgiving, I lingered at the jungle's edge—taking in the gently flowing hills . . . the grass and low bush . . . the blue sky that filled a vast horizon.

Can't be true. It's too good to be true.

Ten days later we arrived on the shores of Lake Albert. It took that long because we had to fight off hordes of local natives who weren't at all happy about the expedition's trespassing on their lands—and weren't about to submit as easily as their slaver-terrorized forest cousins had. As for me, I refused to raise my gun against another human being ever again. The Avisibba had been enough. More than enough. When Lieutenant Stairs looked to me for support in preparing for our first skirmish, I tossed down my rifle and cartridge pouch and held out my empty arms.

"Showing the white feather at this point, Ormsby?" he snarled.

Cowardice had nothing to do with my decision, and Stairs knew it. "Ever heard of the Hippocratic oath, sir?" Parke had enlightened me on a doctor's code of ethics, the solemn vow to cause no harm to one's fellow human beings . . . unfortunately, not till after we'd fought the Avisibba.

"Now you've promoted yourself to doctor?"

I ignored the sneer. "Closest thing we've got here . . . sir."

"Then go hide your head. But prepare for casualties." He raised his stick and whacked at a cowering Zanzibari. "Are you blind? Can't you see the enemy approaching? Ready your weapon!"

But the only casualties were the natives. In such open country, their spears and shields were no competition against the power of our guns. They were sitting ducks. We littered those lovely green grasslands with their bodies. When that wasn't enough, Stairs, Jephson, and their patrols burned to the ground every village in the valley and beyond.

"It is necessary to teach these hostiles a lesson," Stanley proclaimed. "The savage only respects force, power, boldness, and decision."

Flaming agony. We'd turned almost as rotten as the Manyuema. What was left? Cannibalism?

~

Of a sudden we were at Kivalli on the shores of the great lake. Just downwind from Equatoria. Within spitting distance of the beleaguered Emin Pasha at last. About to justify both the suffering and the outrages of the Relief of Emin Pasha Expedition.

Lake Albert came up unexpectedly because it was hidden by a narrow fringe of trees that looked like a ready-made palisade. But the peaceful fishing and salt-making village that was our destination did open onto the shallow expanse of flat, muddy water. None of it was real impressive, but it was the exact spot Stanley'd chosen for his historic rendezvous with the Emin Pasha. The exact spot he'd dictated to the messengers he'd sent up lake to summon the Emin. He'd probably chosen the exact words for greeting the man, too. Stanley'd had lots of time to improve on his famous, "Doctor Livingstone, I presume?" from back in 1871 when he'd found the lost missionary-explorer. The Pasha was supposed to be waiting for us here in Kivalli. A message waited instead.

Stanley read Emin Pasha's letter, then wheeled around to face his remaining officers. "It seems His Excellency is busy at the moment, gentlemen. As he is no longer in need of relief—having vanquished the marauding Mahdists sometime past—the Pasha thanks us for the thought and wishes us well on our return to Zanzibar."

I watched the heat rise on Stanley's face as he crumpled the letter: up his neck, around his ears, across his cheeks, and past his bristling eyebrows.

Stairs tapped his walking stick on the ground. "Damned unsporting of the chap."

Stanley growled long and low. Then he glared at Stairs and Jephson. "Ready yourselves to march the columns back into the forest!"

"*The forest?*" Jephson's voice rose several octaves.

"The forest," Stanley barked. "As the grasslands have proven inhospitable, we will set up an interim camp within the forest's greater security. We cannot afford to waste the Emin Pasha's diminishing supply of ammunition on further skirmishes. Once we successfully contact him, he will be grateful for the gesture. He *will* return with us to Zanzibar—and England. I *will* present him to Queen Victoria herself. Britain *will not* suffer the ignominy of a second Khartoum."

Stanley yanked at his jacket. He took another stab at defending his position.

"The Kivalli canoes aren't worth commandeering for the purpose of making direct contact with the governor of Equatoria at this time; they're not large enough for our needs. It's obvious the *Advance* will be required for the voyage."

Then the orders flew fast.

"Stairs. Once back in the forest, you will trek to Ipoto to collect the boat and our invalids. Jephson. Upon the arrival and rebuilding of the *Advance* on these very shores, you will proceed north to this *Emin Pasha*. You will convince him to present himself to me." Stanley stopped. Another fierce scowl.

"Are my orders quite clear, gentlemen?"

Back to the Great Forest. Bloody misery. If ever there was a cause for mutiny, this was it.

But by now the men were numb. Even Tewfik. He merely shrugged at Stanley's return orders, and with, "It is in Allah's hands," began the long trudge back. We made for Ibwiri, since Stanley hoped to negotiate another expedition stay with Chief Boryo. In an attempt to evade the remaining angry tribes, we took a roundabout route. It didn't help. War cries pursued us, and attacks from the bush felled three of our men. Stanley lost his temper and sent a large party of men ahead to pillage the hostile villages. When they returned with all the poor buggers' cattle, it was feast time again. No surprise when, on December 19, a contingent of natives called from the hills: "The country now lies at your feet! We will hinder you no more!"

The natives may have surrendered, but the weather continued at war. We struggled through a sudden onslaught of cold rains, near up to our waists in mud. Next came a hailstorm. Then there were more hills—these covered with ululating tribesmen, hundreds of them, who we'd robbed of their livelihood. My stomach roiled over the ill-gotten beef it was still digesting. My ears burned with the haunting cries that followed us for miles.

Smoldering Hell. A fine Christian way to spend Christmas Eve.

Christmas day was no improvement. We spent it miserably ferrying bits and pieces of the expedition across the Ituri River on a wobbly banana-stalk raft the porters had built from scratch.

January of 1888 arrived before we sighted Ibwiri once more. It seemed that Chief Boryo and his Balessé had gotten wind of our return. They'd had enough of the expedition, thank you very much. In proof, they'd burned their own comfortable village to the ground and decamped before we could lay eyes on them again. Couldn't blame them, could you? 'Least the fires cut back on the vermin population. Our men also discovered that the Balessé had hedged their bets: in hopes that their village's destruction would send us elsewhere, they'd saved the finest of the house boards from burning and stashed them in the nearby bush. Even better, the Balessé had hastily hidden great stores of Indian corn in that same bush. None of it stayed hidden long.

Obviously feeling that his luck was on the upswing again, Stanley surveyed the ruins of Ibwiri like a conquering hero.

"It will do," he proclaimed to the waiting men. "But from hence Ibwiri will be known as Fort Bodo—*Peaceful* Fort." He clapped his hands. "We will build comfortable huts for all. We will plant Indian corn, beans, and tobacco. There will be food in plenty for my children as we await the *Advance* and our next approach to the Emin Pasha." Another clap. "Chap-chap! Let the building begin!"

Then those idiot Zanzibaris went and cheered the man.

I slunk off into the solitude of the jungle.

Peaceful Fort, my bleeding foot . . . As for the "we," I'd like to see Stanley dirty his hands building and farming. . . . Like to see—

I stopped cold. I'd blundered deeper into the forest than I'd intended. Not a good idea with night coming on. Prickles worked through my spine. Fear sweat followed. . . . Something was stalking me. Something inhuman. I grabbed for my rifle. Too late, I remembered. I'd stopped carrying it in protest of the unending violence.

Scorching pits of Hell. Me and my misplaced sense of ethics. Like to do me in, it was.

I snatched my knife and dropped to my haunches in one smooth movement. Swayed in place, peering through the wild vegetation. There. To my right, about two o'clock and up. *Eyes.* Yellow eyes fixed on me. A low moan escaped. Wasn't me moaning. Was the—

Leopard!

I ducked and rolled as it leaped for me. Split seconds became eternity—eternity enough for admiration of the creature arcing through the air. Sheer grace it was, as the sleek spotted black cat snarled . . . showed off its powerful jaw filled with gleaming daggers of teeth . . . flexed razor-sharp claws ready for the kill. I raised my blade for the hopeless struggle—

And a net caught the beast in mid-air.

I did another flip before the falling cat crushed me, then bounded to my feet.

"Kenge," I whispered. "You? Here?"

A single arrow slid into the leopard's throat. It writhed . . . and stilled. Only then did my Pygmy friends converge on me and their prize.

"Fito!"

Kenge beamed as I swooped him up into an enormous hug. A flood of excited chatter followed, the gist of it being that I was more useful for leopard hunting than any beating of the bush or any trap. I grinned. Here was another career option for me: sacrificial goat. I set Kenge down.

"Why are you and your people here?"

"Why have you returned?"

Our questions barreled into each other. Obviously there was much to discuss, much conversation to enjoy. Stanley and Fort Bodo—all my cares—dissolved as I joined my Pygmy friends' celebratory march to their traveling camp.

I returned to Fort Bodo two mornings later sporting a necklace of wicked claws. I barely had a moment to take in the stockade growing around the encampment, when a frantic Jephson pounced on me with the hunger of my late leopard.

"Where have you been?" he screeched. "Stairs left for Ipoto and Stanley is sick!"

"What are his symptoms?" I automatically asked.

"A frightful stomach and a frightful temper!"

Jephson was right on both counts. The stomach business looked like acute gastritis to me. I dealt with it the best I knew how, severely limiting Stanley's diet to the softest, blandest foods. Worse still, the man had a nasty abscessed arm. I figured that was the real root of his problems. He fought me tooth and nail while I tried to clean it up. At last I had to calm him with morphia. That's when I got a better look at the wound.

Blast. Seemed as if one of his blood-brother slashes had gone bad. Must've been festering for ages. Could it be the one from that villain Ismaili in Ipoto? I felt for my Pygmy scars. They'd healed nicely, giving me a rather rakish look. A new surge of warmth for Kenge—and the wisdom of his people's medicine—overtook me. Had to get the recipe for that little pot of ashy black *dawa* the next time we met. Whenever that might be. For the here and now, I was stuck with Stanley.

The great explorer was not an easy patient, even after we moved him into the roomy whitewashed clay "headquarters" building raised for him. Jephson and I shared the nursing honors, but Jephson got the better end of the deal. I was trying not to overdo the morphia, but gave Stanley a shot at bedtime when Jephson took over for the night. That left me imprisoned with our feverish leader during the day.

Stanley lapsed in and out of consciousness. And when he awoke, it was with a vengeance. His servant boy, Sali, was bright enough to disappear indefinitely, doing "laundry." Aside from the rats, I was the only soul about. So Stanley fixated on me. His voice switching from an American twang to a Welsh singsong like it did when he was upset, he went into tirades about my service, even my character. Had no reason to do that, did he? Yet Stanley called me impetuous, rash, and spoiled rotten. Then he went on about his own superior character.

"I was a bit impetuous and rash at your age myself, Ormsby," he admitted. "But I learned to curb my temper"—this with a straight face—"studied wisdom . . . adopted patience."

"Indeed, sir." No point debating with a madman, was there? "Just let me change the dressing on your arm, if you will." I reached for it—

"No!" Stanley screeched. "I've had enough of your insolence! Enough of your playing at doctor!"

Quicker than I'd thought possible, he leaped from his sickbed, grabbed his stick, and attacked me with it. Too late, I blocked my head. *Where'd the man get the strength to give me such a crack? Bleeding agony. Wasn't it enough I had to nurse him every day for weeks? I was supposed to take his abuse, too?*

I ducked the next blow and rose with an uppercut to Stanley's chin that would've made Chief Engineer Alexander McNabb proud. Good and properly dazed, Stanley toppled nicely onto his cot. I reached for the morphia needle. Why should Jephson have the sole benefit of overseeing a subdued Henry Morton Stanley?

Only after watching the drug drain into his veins, after seeing the twitch and sigh of pleasure that came with its oblivion, did I risk checking the man's arm. It'd been coming along nicely, but those whacks had opened the wound again. *Bloody Hell.* I dug in my bag for the sewing kit. Now I'd have to stitch the whole thing up and start over again. Luckily Mum had given me a few sewing lessons—"just sufficient to save a button and mend the odd tear, our Tom"—before my fateful embarkation. *Mercy.* Mum never had a clue.

Ignoring the steady throb in my head from Stanley's blow, I carefully threaded a needle. Parke couldn't get here soon enough.

Surgeon T. H. Parke finally turned up at Fort Bodo in the middle of February with Stairs's caravan from Ipoto. The first thing he did was walk through the door of Stanley's quarters: same drooping mustache, same unkempt hair, same sad eyes.

"Doc! Thank God you're here!"

"I share your sentiments, Tom." He raised an eyebrow at my scars and necklace, gave me a quick clap on the back, then bent over the dozing Stanley. "I think."

I drew him away and quietly gave him a rundown of my patient's history. Paused. "He's all yours, Doc. I'm due for a little relief of my own."

Outside, I squinted through the midday sun till I got my bearings. I spotted Nelson first. He slumped in the dust of Fort Bodo's main street right alongside the *Advance*'s steel sections, where the porters had dumped the lot. The captain hadn't gained back any of his lost years at Ipoto. Not much of his lost hair, either. I nodded at him, then at Stairs, rocking with exhaustion nearby. By rights I should've offered succor and support then and there, but being in need of a little succor and support myself, I hastened to make my escape.

Barely ten yards from Stanley's quarters, I heard our noble leader bark for Lieutenant Stairs. Teetering with indecision—and, truth be told, curiosity—I stayed planted under the hot sun. Stayed planted long enough to watch Stairs take a deep breath and limp past me into the lion's den. Long enough to hear the low murmurs of protest spreading over the camp as Stanley roused himself sufficiently to order the officer and his spent porters to return to the road directly.

This time Stairs was to backtrack even farther, all the way to Ugarrowwa's slave fortress to collect our remaining porters. Here was Stanley with his precious boat back, but no strength to escort the *Advance* out of the forest and down to Lake Albert. Plenty of strength to take out his ire on one of his last useful officers, though. I shook my head.

Got to get out. Got to get away for a few days. I'll be next on the madman's agenda. For a cert.

Where to hide? I turned toward the Great Forest. Studied its inviting depths. Would Kenge and his people still be waiting?

This time I was bound and determined to re-enter the jungle prepared. I had my rifle and cartridges. I had a packet of food. And I had Tewfik.

"Think well, my brother," he said, when I asked him to join me. He pointed to my forehead. "Has not the Great Forest already marked you for life?"

"All the more reason for you to join me." I grinned. "So it does not mark me for death."

"Bull Boy, Bull Boy." He sighed a heartfelt sigh. "Pray Allah your obstinacy does not overwhelm your strength." A shrug of a shoulder. "Perhaps the Gardens of Heaven will be opened to one who befriended an innocent infidel."

I laughed. "It's only for a few days, Tewfik. I must get the smell of Stanley's sickbed out of my nostrils."

"Ho," he grunted. "And the smell of the master, too, I think." He nodded at the angry welt still competing with the scars on my forehead.

I'd never mentioned my patient's outrages to a soul, but

the camp knew. It knew everything.

"Less said."

We entered the Great Forest.

Kenge's traveling camp was deserted, but a message had been left for me. The perfectly cured head of a leopard was jauntily posed upon a stake in the center of the camp. I circled it, then forced myself to check the charred remains of the cook fires. The Pygmies had been gone for at least a week, much too long for me to catch up with them. I must be satisfied with their parting gift.

Their gift. *Wonder of wonders.* The great cat's jaws were spread wide in a toothy, ferocious snarl. Its eye sockets had been drilled open. A mask? I tentatively fit the skull over my head . . . peered at the world through the leopard's eyes. . . . The clack of drumsticks on hollow logs filled my brain. My feet followed the rhythm, breaking into a stalking dance around the dead fires. I slunk into a crouch, ready to let out a deep moan, ready to spread my claws and pounce—

"In Allah's name!" Tewfik cried. "What is this wish you have to become a godless savage?"

Gradually I stilled my feet. As the drumbeats faded from my mind, I stretched upright and pulled off the leopard mask. With regret. Great regret. The world had looked different from behind it. It had looked like the Pygmies' world of *Ndura.* "Never ask me to explain this mystery, my brother. I cannot."

I strapped the mask to my back and we moved on.

On the third day in the forest, I left Tewfik asleep inside the Pygmy-style shelter we'd built and walked in silence to a nearby stream for my ablutions. Early morning mists shaped and reshaped the trees, the creepers, even the lowly mushrooms. The very air had a curious tingle to it. I squatted and reached out a hand to cup the water . . . and stopped in mid-act. I was being stalked again. No . . . observed. Letting my hand drop, I slowly raised my eyes. Hidden in the foliage across the stream was a face. A familiar face. Where had I seen it before? The memory returned. My night of horrors in Ipoto . . . the medicine man with his moon mask and great monkey topknot—

More miracles. Soko. A great ape. A gorilla. Alive.

She—it was a she, for a sleepy baby clung to her back— stared at me with as much fascination as I had with her. I smiled . . . and she returned the smile. Next she called out a low hoot. I sent the hoot back. My new friend considered. Then she took a careful step away from shelter and majestically approached her side of the stream. Squatting like me, she reached out a huge hand to cup the water. I mirrored her. We drank.

"Brother, brother! Where are you?"

Not now, Tewfik, I prayed.

Too late. He crashed through the jungle, near bowling me over into the stream.

"In Heaven's name!" He caught me, caught himself. "What is that?"

I slowly rose. My new-made friend was already high in the canopy. Safe. "What *was* that. That was a gorilla, Tewfik. A gorilla and its child."

Tewfik the Bold trembled. "Forgive me. I have not your taste for these things. Have not your taste for the jungle."

A weary sigh spread though me. "You have not, for a cert." I took his arm. "Come, my brother, it is time to return to 'civilization.' I think the Great Forest has just given me its last gift."

THE DOLDRUMS

MY SPIRITS WERE SINKING LOWER BY THE DAY.
Stanley wasn't well enough to return to Lake Albert with the
Advance, but he was well enough to issue orders. When he com-
manded patrols to systematically wipe out what he called the
"dwarf" villages around us, I fervently protested to the mighty
explorer himself. Principles were principles. A fellow had to stand
up for his friends.

"Stop!" he ordered in the midst of my pleas. "Your dwarfs—"

"People of the *Ndura*," I boldly corrected. "The rightful
inhabitants of the Great Forest."

"—Are hostiles. With poison arrows—and stockpiles of plantains. Hostiles cannot be countenanced within our territory, and
their food is needed to see Fort Bodo through its first harvests."

"But it's *their* territory. It's *their* food, and they need it, too."

Stanley's eyebrows twitched, and a telltale red began coloring
his cheeks. "I seem to recall that you were taken on as a 'general
dogsbody,' Ormsby. Questioning authority does not become you.
Leave that to your superiors in future."

I spent the following weeks at Fort Bodo spitting mad and power-less to do aught about it. *Flaming misery.* As if the Pygmies and their way of life were a threat to the expedition. More like the other way 'round, wasn't it? It gave me some solace knowing that Kenge and his people were too smart to get caught. But they were also too smart to linger around Fort Bodo. I mourned their absence, lived in my leopard necklace, and sullenly bided my time.

Not waiting for Stairs to return, Henry Morton Stanley dragged the rest of us from out the forest and back to the muddy lakeshore in mid-April. When the moment arrived for him to pick a crew for the *Advance*'s voyage to the Emin Pasha—currently believed to be at his Mswa station uplake—I made good and sure I was in the boat with Parke and Jephson, the fifteen rowers, and the comple-ment of fifty men. Fifty men for what? Security? To impress the Emin Pasha with the sorry remains of Stanley's expedition? Small matter. As we cast off, I sat in the boat grinning my fool head off. Parke turned his attention from the receding encampment to me.

"Care to share the joke, Tom? Humor's been in nearly as short a supply as food of late."

"A rare thrill, Doc. Leaving Stanley high and dry on the shores of Lake Albert while we make the two-day trip to Mswa. Only think on it. We get to lay eyes on his Holy Grail, this Emin Pasha fellow—"

"Before Henry Morton Stanley!" Parke exclaimed.

Next thing you know, we were both grinning like idiots. When Jephson scowled at us from his captain's post at the bow, we began to laugh. I would've slapped my sides and rolled flat out like Kenge, but upsetting the crammed boat into the jaws of the wait-ing crocs wasn't on my agenda.

We arrived at the Emin's closest station on April 23, to be told that His Excellency, the governor of the Equatorial Province, was on an inspection tour of his other seven stations and would return in due course. After what greeted us in Mswa, I didn't care how long he delayed his return.

Never laid eyes on such sleek Nubian guards and well-fed servants—all dressed in the freshest cotton robes! Never imagined the world still held such clean quarters and lice-free beds! To top it all off, these people of Emin Pasha's treated me like an officer!

I'd barely stumbled off our boat when I was escorted to my own whitewashed hut. Hardly turned round and a servant brought me lunch: an omelet made from more eggs than I'd seen since leaving England, real bread, and butter . . . *bloody miracles*! I polished off the food, then tested the bed. When I awoke, it was to more miracles. Sitting smack in the middle of the room was a tub full of crystal-clear hot water! With real soap! Even one of those Egyptian loofah things to scrub with. I whooped a mighty whoop and dove in.

Suddenly Parke was at the door, looking considerably cleaner himself.

"You all right, Tom?"

I sent a splash of water at him. "Ever consider we might've been on the wrong end of the expedition all this time, Doc?"

He laughed and left me to my bath. Wasn't till I'd contended with months of layered dirt and stood dripping before a wicker bureau that I made my next discovery.

Bleeding mercy, I'd started a beard.

I stared at the blond wisps in the mirror set atop the bureau. Stared some more. I'd become a man with options! I considered them carefully, with due gravity. . . . Could try for a walrus mustache like Stanley and every last one of his officers. But did I really want to look more like a white conqueror than I already did? . . . . Then again, I could go for a chin beard on the order of Tewfik's. I stroked my chin. Hadn't any spare fat, but the bones'd thickened up some, squared out more than I'd remembered. Turned my head this way and that, hunting for the best profile. No question, it was a good, solid chin that didn't need any hiding.

I reached for the shaving gear that'd been left out for me, tentatively wet the thick brush, dunked it into its pot of soap, and lathered my bronzed cheeks. Made a few faces in the mirror like our dad used to do. Finally I sprang open the straight razor. Clean-shaven is how Tom Ormsby would face the world. What's the point of having a good, honest face, and a good, solid square chin—not to mention a forehead full of good, genuine Pygmy scars—and cover 'em all up?

Grinning at my lathered image in the mirror, I wielded the razor.

Our fifty Zanzibaris were finally put to use. Standing with rifles at ease, they flanked Mswa's ceremonial square, adding appropriate pomp as the Emin Pasha presented himself at last. I stared as he and Jephson confronted each other.

Mercy.

The man I'd sacrificed nearly two years of my life for wasn't any titan in the flesh. He wasn't aught but a tall, frail-looking fellow in a *dishdash* and thick spectacles. He had a neatly trimmed dark beard filling out his hollow cheeks, and his high, narrow forehead disappeared under a fez. Now his eyes set into a squint as Jephson droned through Stanley's ultimatums.

"Henry Morton Stanley sends his best wishes and requests that you return immediately with your steamboat to consult with him. He suggests you bring rations sufficient to subsist his expedition while all await your removal. Say, about twelve thousand to fifteen thousand pounds of grain . . . "

I was too mortified to do aught but stand at attention. Mind you, I stood at attention in my new boots, trousers, shirt, and jacket provided by the Emin Pasha's largesse. Even new underwear. All tailored to my body by the Emin Pasha's seamstresses and shoemakers. For a cert, the boots'd come in the very nick. My old soles had thinned too close to the tapeworm-bearing ground.

I glanced stiffly down at the spit-and-polish shine on my well-clad feet, thinking over the last few days. I'd spent them exploring part of the governor's domain. It was enough to embarrass any right-thinking member of the Relief of Emin Pasha Expedition. Far from being on the verge of extinction, the Emin'd gathered around him near fifteen thousand followers: some the necessary soldiers and bureaucrats, true, but also natives who'd flocked to his humane care. His lands were prosperous with plantations, neat villages, happy and safe people. His workshops produced anything and everything he and his charges needed. Proper titan or no, the man *was* a wonder—a just and intelligent ruler in the middle of a continent gone mad.

The Emin lifted his hand to halt Jephson's whine and finally spoke: "I shall consider all things your Mr. Stanley proposes. If you will be kind enough to excuse me for the moment? I have been away too long. It is necessary first that I attend to my affairs here."

It was perfectly fine English, but with a German accent. Having said his piece, he strode purposefully away, leaving a wilting Jephson to dismiss all those Zanzibaris, and Parke and me very much in the lurch. I turned to the surgeon.

"England's sent this entire expedition to save a *German?*"

"A German mercenary in the pay of the Egyptian puppet government, which happens to be under the British protectorate." Doc shrugged. "While you've been roaming around Mswa, I've been picking up intelligence from Captain Casuti, his Italian aide-de-camp. It seems Emin Pasha was born Edward Schnitzer of Jewish parents in Prussia some forty-eight years ago. The man is a linguist and a medical doctor—"

"A doctor?" I cried.

"Indeed." Parke watched the Emin's slightly hunched figure as he escaped down the palm-lined street into his headquarters building. "He worked with Gordon at Khartoum well before its fall. They called him 'Emin Effendi Hakim,' the faithful physician."

A whistle slipped through my lips.

"Wait." Parke's eyes lit up with rare glee. "You haven't heard the best part."

"What else can this marvel do?"

"Our Emin Pasha also happens to be a rabid botanist, not to mention a student of entomology—insects, to you—"

"Doc! You two ought to get along like a house on fire!"

Parke sobered. "If I can get past Stanley and this farce of a relief expedition."

I studied my new togs some more. They'd take breaking in, they would. Still creased with starch instead of grime. "Wouldn't mind getting past them myself."

Emin Pasha's people called it a smoke boat, but his eighty-five-foot steamer, the *Khedive*, wasn't aught to sneer at. Leaving the *Advance* behind, the Emin and the rest of us boarded her the next day. She paddle wheeled away from Mswa's dock under the power of the best-kept boilers I'd encountered in the entire Congo. I wanted the trip through the golden light of late afternoon to last forever. Wanted to keep leaning on the railing like a tourist again, watching the colors change on the gently rippling water, watching the pods of hippos yawn and snort and lumber into the marshes for their night feeds, quick-footed egrets trailing them. But the *Khedive* retraced the *Advance*'s two-day trip in two hours flat.

My brief vacation ended as we dropped anchor in the deeper waters off Badzwa, Stanley's new lakeshore camp. Just after the equatorial sun slammed into blackness, it was. I clambered from the torch-lit launch as Stanley shepherded the Emin Pasha into his tent. Meanwhile the expedition's Zanzibaris wasted a little more of the Emin's ammunition, firing wild, celebratory shots into the night. I couldn't help snorting like one of those hippos.

"What was that remarking upon, Tom?"

Parke had caught up with me from behind. "Stanley's finally going to get to drink those five bottles of champagne he's been hoarding since Stanley Pool."

Doc patted my shoulder consolingly. "Cheer up, old chap. They're bound to have gone flat by this time."

Like the champagne's bubbles, the fizz disappeared fast from Stanley and the Emin Pasha's relationship. They talked under a canvas canopy erected outside the expedition's headquarters on the shores of Lake Albert. And talked some more, till it sounded closer to fighting to me. For a cert, I was in a position to know.

Tom Ormsby, majordomo, was on call for any little thing the two might need-another cup of tea? A light for Stanley's endless cigars? A fresh boy to whisk away the surrounding marsh's mosquitoes and flies? The job gave me plenty of opportunity to study both men. To notice that Stanley made a point of keeping the negotiations at camp-chair level. Wouldn't do for the Emin's extra inches to tower over Bula Matari, would it?

After a week of meetings, the Emin still refused to abandon his people to the mercy of enemy tribes—and was realistic enough to understand the nightmare of marching the lot to the sea and Zanzibar.

"My good sir," Emin Pasha explained. "I am responsible for fifty Egyptian officers and fifteen hundred Soudanese soldiers. Then one must take into account their wives, concubines, children, and servants . . . some ten thousand human beings. Only consider the logistics! And then there are my five thousand faithful natives. Are they to be abandoned unprotected?"

It was fair obvious Stanley didn't give a fig about any of that. All he wanted was a tame Emin Pasha to show off in England, just like he'd done with Baruti.

"I must reiterate, must once more ask you to keep in mind, Emin, that the khedive of Egypt has made it brutally clear he has no further interest in Equatoria. No further relief will be sent. You—and your people—will stay on at your own risk."

Stanley's temper built. The final straw was when the Emin

thanked him yet again for the thirty-one loads of ammunition that'd actually made it into the governor's hands. As if this subtle insult wasn't enough, he added, "But my dear Mr. Stanley, more ammunition isn't really critical. *I* must reiterate that the situation in my province is currently quite stable."

"Have it your way!" Stanley roared, charging from the chair opposite his opponent. "Enough time has been wasted on fruitless talk. I've a missing rear column to rescue in Yambuya!" He tugged at his jacket and tried mightily for a breath to swallow his choler. "But in six months, six months, good sir"—the Welsh singsong took over—"we will have a rendezvous at this very spot. In the interim it is your duty to present evacuation as an option to your people. Go or stay, I expect a rational decision from you at that time."

As the Emin stalked off, Stanley bellowed for his officers. Since they'd been skulking nearby trying to follow the ups and downs of the negotiations, it didn't take them long to present themselves.

"Jephson, you are to remain with the Emin."

One thing you could say about Henry Morton Stanley: *he* didn't have any problems making on-the-spot decisions.

"In case of unforeseen difficulties, you are responsible for guiding him and his entourage to Zanzibar. Parke!"

Doc shrugged to attention. "Mr. Stanley?"

"In Stairs's absence, it falls upon you to prepare the men for our return to Fort Bodo. The Emin is kindly loaning us one hundred thirty porters to ease us on our way." He shifted to me. "Ormsby, as your current duties are no longer required, assist Parke. Chap-chap!"

On the first day's march back toward the Great Forest, nearly all of the borrowed porters deserted. Stanley promptly sent a letter of complaint by messenger to the Emin. The second day, Stanley made the next great geographical discovery of his career: he spotted a peak of the legendary Mountains of the Moon rising through a heavy cover of clouds in the distance. Halting the caravan, he hauled out his aneroid, took altitude measurements, and decided the range was the missing source of the Nile. He promptly sent another letter by messenger to the Emin as a sort of official publication of this coup. 'Course, Stanley neglected to mention that Parke and I had spotted that selfsame peak while off for a walk the week before. We'd duly plotted it and reported our sighting to Stanley, only to be pooh-poohed. Now Doc and I watched the messenger make tracks for the lake.

"Guess there won't be any Mount Ormsby on the next batch of African maps." I sighed. "My mum'll have to live with the disappointment."

Parke gazed mournfully at the far-off range as the cloudbank slowly enveloped the peak once more. "There won't be any Mount Parke, either." He shoved at his lank hair. "To the perceived victor belongs the spoils."

Back at Fort Bodo, Stairs had returned from Ugarrawwa's fortress with the porters we'd left behind. Nelson was looking a tad healthier. Stanley didn't waste any time admiring either them or the camp. By mid-June, he'd gotten together a new caravan to search for the missing Barttelot—and, more importantly by Stanley's lights—our missing supplies. The caravan consisted of 113 Zanzibaris, 95 porters sent by the Emin to replace those who'd deserted beyond Lake Albert, 4 of the Emin's soldiers to keep them in hand, Stanley—and me.

"Why *me?*" I groused to Tewfik.

Tewfik carefully lifted and balanced a new load upon his head. "Why you? Why *me?* It is as Allah wills. Our bodies are strong enough for this new burden."

"But are our spirits?"

His only answer was a shrug.

I spent my eighteenth birthday digging up buried ammunition at a place I'd hoped—prayed, even—never to set eyes on again: Starvation Camp. After that, the trek became nothing more than a litany of near-forgotten horrors.

—"Skewers!"

—"Pitfall to the right!"

—"Beware thorns!"

—"'Ware nettles! . . .'Ware choking creepers!"

—"Look sharp for ants! Red ants a'march!"

No brightly feathered birds crossed my path. No game silently stalked me from the bush. There was nothing but swarms of mosquitoes and dust—dust beneath my feet, dust before my eyes, dust fighting with mosquitoes for space to clog my mouth and nose.

Blast it all. No sane human being deserved this torture more than once.

Then there were the evenings spent with Stanley. As the only other European in the party, I'd half expected to be invited to his table, despite our differences of opinion. The man had to have some kind of human urge to share a little conversation at the end of a long day's march, right?

Wrong.

Seems I couldn't get one simple fact into my head: I was still a mere ranker, still socially beyond the pale.

Oh, the master desired me at his table right enough—cleaned up and playing the majordomo again. 'Least that solved the mystery of why he chose me for the trek. I stood at attention with my jaw clamped shut till it fair ached, waiting for his nod. Then, with a pristine linen napkin folded over my left arm and with the grace of a ballet dancer, I silently waited on an equally silent Henry Morton Stanley. That chore accomplished, I dined with Tewfik. He was better company any way you looked at it.

We covered a respectable 460 miles in two months and were only 80 miles short of Yambuya when we found the rear column of the

Relief of Emin Pasha Expedition at last. Blundered on it, more like—or what was left of it. The remainder of our missing porters lay dying behind the palisades of the Ituri River village of Banalya. I pray Heaven I'll never stumble upon another such charnel house again.

Flaming torture. Starvation Camp should've toughened me up some.

Smallpox had struck the carriers wrested from Tippu-Tib. Inoculation'd saved our men from that scourge, only to have starvation lay them low. Mr. William Bonny was the sole expedition member wandering upright through the disaster of putrid, unburied bodies. I had to wrap a cloth around my nose and mouth to venture close enough to hear his tale of woe as Stanley marched forward to accost him.

"Where is Major Barttelot?" Stanley barked.

Amazing how he could skip right past the simple courtesy of a greeting and maybe a show of sympathy for the complete catastrophe surrounding us.

Bonny stiffened within his ragged uniform like a good soldier. "The major is dead, sir."

"Good God! How, dead? Fever?"

"No, sir, he was shot."

"By whom?"

"By the Manyuema."

The shortest of pauses on Stanley's part.

"Where is Jameson?"

"At Stanley Falls."

"What is he doing there?"

"He went to obtain more porters from Tippu-Tib. Sir."

"Well, then," Stanley pressed, "where is Mr. Ward or Mr. Troup?"

"Mr. Ward is at Bangala, and Mr. Troup was invalided home some months ago."

"And Mr. Walker?"

"Long since returned to Leopoldville. Said as how his job was finished after he escorted the empty steamers back to Stanley Pool."

And so it went while our Zanzibaris prowled through the chaos to learn who among their long-lost comrades still lived. There were a few cries of joy, but many more howls of grief.

Stanley got over Barttelot's death and the other unwanted news fast. His interrogation completed, he clapped his hands. Ever true to form, Bula Matari's orders followed immediately: "The living will bury the dead. The well will care for the sick. After we gather our plundered supplies, we will evacuate Banalya for healthier land upriver. Chap-chap!"

I can't say that Mr. William Bonny and I ever saw eye to eye on anything. But that first night the rough old drill sergeant and I banded together around a campfire with our tin plates of stewed plantains. Guess it was a sort of mutual recognition of the fact that we were both mere rankers, both socially beyond the pale, both excluded from Stanley's company even after all we'd accomplished.

I swallowed a mushy mouthful. "Wish it had a dash of sugar."

He swallowed in turn. "Syrup'd go down considerable better. Lyle's Golden Syrup. And a pint of porter. Hell, I'd trade 'em all for a good bottle of whiskey."

We both sighed.

"Here now." I finally bit the bullet. "What really happened back in Yambuya? What really happened to Barttelot?"

Bonny snorted. "The major went sheer, raving starkers, is what happened. Near from the beginning. First it was while waiting on the steamboats to come back upriver." He swiped at his grizzled mustache gone gray. "Take the food situation."

I raised a questioning eyebrow.

"Our rations disappeared real quick. And you know how he never did take to the blacks, any of 'em, even our own people?"

I knew. Only multiply by a hundred or so Barttelot's sneers at the likes of me and Bonny, add a ready whip, and the picture became too clear. I nodded.

"Stands to reason the local natives had no mind to trade food with the man, blood brother or no. So right off he gets this bright idea—force 'em to trade."

I set down my fork. "How?"

"Fair clever it was, I'll hand him that. What could be easier than kidnapping a few women and children and holding 'em for ransom?"

I stared at my unfinished food in the fire's flickering light. A plateful of termites couldn't have looked worse. "That's all?"

"All? You mean aside from flogging the odd Zanzibari to death at his whim? And shackling the others, like they was his slaves? And feuding with his officers till any civil conversation was killed dead? And letting Tippu-Tib play him for the fool month after month?"

Bonny wielded his spoon like a bayonet as he sliced into his plantains. "Can't tell you how many trips Barttelot made to the blasted slaver's headquarters in Stanley Falls, begging for the porters the villain'd promised Stanley so we could move forward from Yambuya at last. 'Course that's after the steamers finally arrived upriver with the last lot of supplies—"

"At least," I interrupted, "that should've improved the food situation."

This time Bonny spat. Carefully, with a trooper's aplomb, straight into the fire. "Damn me if it did. Wasn't but beads and bangles and more ammunition."

"Barttelot didn't take it well," I guessed.

He laughed a cruel, heartless laugh. "Ordered Ward clear back to Banana and beyond to find the first telegraph he could to send a complaint to the expedition governors in London."

"Not a rational decision."

"Rational?" This time Bonny hooted. "How'd you think he got himself murdered? Right here in Banalya, but a month past?"

I took the bait. "How?"

"Barttelot'd finally got a handful of porters out of Tippu-Tib,"—Bonny pointed beyond the fire—"that lot we buried from the smallpox. The wily slaver bastard must've known they was infected, right? So the major and me was resting up here for the night,"—he pointed again—"that's the very vermin-infested hut, plague take it. The Manyuema's stockpile of ivory was piled right next to it. Couple tons of it—which is long gone, more's the pity."

"Wait a minute. The Manyuema are in Tippu-Tib's pay, too? Not just Kilonga-Longa's and Ugarrawwa's?"

"Lots of Manyuema out there, boy. They do their dirty work for the highest bidder."

My turn to sigh. *Why couldn't the Pygmies be in charge instead?*

Bonny carried on. "The Manyuema running the village were having one of their little parties. Nothing out of the usual . . . the sheer-naked painted bodies, the masks—"

"Masks?" I shuddered.

"The drums, the dancing, the lot. It goes on long after we've packed it in, well into the wee hours . . . when of a sudden Barttelot bounds from his cot—had to bunk with him, didn't I? The man needed a keeper. So there he is, leaping like he's got the Saint Vitus's dance, and screaming, 'The drums! Stop the drums!'"

Bonny downed another bite of his food. "Before I could catch him, he'd gone and grabbed his revolver and was out of the hut like a shot. By the time I'd yanked on my boots, the madman was aiming that gun dead on at a naked lady drummer. Wailing like a banshee, he was. 'Stop the drums! Stop the drums! Stop them, or I swear I'll shoot!'"

I blinked. "Then what?"

Bonny shrugged. "The lady's husband shot *him* dead through the heart."

"Oh."

"Then the party went on, and I buried Barttelot."

Didn't need my queasy stomach to tell me I'd heard enough. I offered my plantain mush to Bonny. "Have room for a second helping?"

"After what I been through?" He snatched at the food.

"Waste not, want not," I mumbled, and lurched for my tent.

On August 30, 1888, the reconstituted expedition began its journey back to Fort Bodo. It took four months this time, and the trek was near as bad as the first crossing of the Great Forest. When we limped through the palisade gates on December 20, we'd lost another 106 men through starvation, sickness, and hostile attacks. Only got through it myself by near turning into an automaton. Taking one step after another . . . blindly swallowing one grub after another. Wasn't any bush or jungle or forest. Wasn't aught but an endless Hell that Pastor Gribbins's fire-and-brimstone sermons couldn't come near to describing.

Never forgetting the second time Mr. William Bonny took me into his confidence. Another one of those brooding jungle nights, it was. Heaviness pressed like a ton-weight over the camp. Lightning toyed at the edges of the canopy.

"Ormsby!"

Bonny waylaid me after my evening duties with Stanley, beckoning me with a gourd. Its stench hit me as I closed in.

"Palm wine!"

Bonny swallowed a gulp. "No cause to sneer. Ain't whiskey, like Jameson's family makes back in Ireland, but it's got its merits." He backed into a huge banyan tree and slumped down along one of its roots. "C'mere." He patted a hollow in the trunk next to him. "Have a snort with me. This pestilential jungle does things to a man. Need to get it off your chest once in a while."

Hard to disagree with that, wasn't it? I slumped down next to him. Thunder sounded in the distance like native drums. Bonny lifted the wine to his lips again.

"Plaguey drums. Night like this, can't get 'em out of my head."

He passed the gourd.

I took a sip and shivered. "It's the masks that do for me," I confessed.

"Them, too. I calls 'em the Revenge of the Heathen. They know how to get inside a white man . . . and squeeze."

I was still gripping the wine and went for another taste. Just to chase away the image of those leering masks, mind you. "They seem to have done for Barttelot, right enough."

"Hah. You ain't heard nothing. Pass back that wine, boy."

Helped myself to an extra swallow first, just in case. "Here now. What could be worse than Barttelot going crazy?"

Silence while Bonny drank deeply. Then, "Jameson *not* going crazy."

I rested my head against the banyan's smooth bark. A little palm wine went a long way. "What d'you mean?"

Bonny tugged at an ear. "Just a few months back it was, with Jameson on one of them hopeless missions trying to come to terms with Tippu-Tib . . . laying over with the slaver for the night at one of his Manyuema villages—Riba-Riba."

"What happened there . . . with Jameson?"

A quick slug from the gourd, like Bonny needed its strength. "The local chief decides to put on a proper party in Tippu-Tib's honor. So there they all are, feasting away the night . . . more of the usual naked heathen entertainments taking place to the usual heathen jungle music . . . and out of the blue Jameson turns to the slaver.

"'Tippu-Tib, what do these dancers call themselves?'

"'The Wacusi. They are cousins to the Manyuema and, like them, are cannibals.'

"Jameson goes and sniffs one of them superior sniffs, like he does. 'It's hard for a chap to believe these people are really cannibals. I mean, my word . . .'"

Bonny raised the wine to his mouth again. "Then Tippu-Tib smiles his sly smile. 'Only make them a gift of a few pieces of cloth.' So Jameson sends his boy for six handkerchiefs and they change hands. . . ."

By this time my eyes were closed and the celebration at Riba-Riba floated before me. Could see the clay-daubed dancers, could hear the drums and flutes, the wild chants. "What happened next?"

"Next? A Wacusi appears, leading a young slave girl by the hand. The bloke stops by the fire, gives the child a comforting nod, like everything's on the up and up . . . and stabs her through the heart with his knife."

My head banged against the tree. Hard.

Bonny's flat, gruff voice relentlessly spewed the rest of the story into the night. "Three more blighters rush up and chop her to pieces, saving the head for last. Then, quick as you please, in she goes to the closest cook pot—"

I grabbed for the wine and near drained the gourd. Next I reeled over and hurled it all out.

"*Damn!*" Bonny snatched back the gourd and shook it. "Near empty. No cause to waste it that-aways!"

I swiped at my mouth and sat up. "Proof. What proof do you have?"

He squinted at me. "Why, Jameson himself. Swear on my regiment, he wasn't jiggering me." Bonny sucked in his breath, then slowly exhaled, like maybe the old drill sergeant was wishing he was still browbeating recruits in some saner part of the empire. "He made sketches of the lot. Showed 'em off to me. Pleased as punch, he was, with his 'anthro . . . anthro-po-log-ical . . . ob-ser-vations. . . .'"

Bonny paused, cradling the gourd. Belched. "Almost as proud of them pictures as of that savage warrior's head he salted and shipped home for stuffing after one of our skirmishes."

Mercy. The final straw at last. And yet—

I struggled to my knees. "Did he . . . did Jameson *eat* the girl?"

The thunder had turned into enormous bass drums. A bolt of lightning honed in on us. Mr. William Bonny drained the last of the wine and tossed the gourd into the coming storm. "He'd bought and paid for her, hadn't he? As for tasting the goods . . . that he never did say."

When the rear column of the Relief of Emin Pasha Expedition staggered into Fort Bodo, I was so worn down, it almost seemed like home. Stanley gave us two days to acclimate, then marched the entire complement back out of the forest and down to Lake Albert for the last time. He was two months late for his rendezvous with Emin Pasha.

Little matter. The Emin'd had his hands full, too. When he presented Stanley's directive to vacate the province, the governor's Egyptian officers had mutinied with intentions of ruling the lucrative Equatoria themselves. The Emin and Jephson were taken hostage. Next the Mahdists swooped south from the Soudan to launch yet another *jihad*. This was a brand-new holy war like the one that'd wiped out Gordon at Khartoum. Like the earlier attack on the Emin that'd launched our mission from England. Because of this new crisis, the Emin and Jephson were released, and the governor made a tentative peace with his officers. But beset on all sides and with his utopia shattered—thanks in great part to Stanley's "rescue"—the Emin Pasha found himself with no choice. He was joining Henry Morton Stanley's relief expedition to Zanzibar after all.

THE MARCH TO THE SEA

FEBRUARY 17, 1889. UNDER THE ESCORT OF officers and soldiers who'd remained faithful, the Emin Pasha and a small party of sixty-five arrived by land caravan at Kivalli camp on the marshy shores of Lake Albert. But his ex-excellency still hesitated over the final leave-taking. There were more families to gather from stations along the Nile. There was more scientific data to enter into his endless note-books, more specimens to collect. It was this fanatic curiosity that irritated Stanley the most. Each morning the Emin sent out his clerk, Rajab, to shoot every bird or animal he could find. The Emin would receive these offerings, lovingly caress them, then order: "Skin them immediately!"

By night the creatures would be hanging in suspension, stuffed with cotton. A few days later, they'd be packed for the British Museum.

Stanley's annoyance grew. "I suspect our Pasha would have a greater affection for *my* bleached skull and bones. I'll not give him the pleasure."

The rift between the adventurer and the thinker kept getting deeper. I'll say this for Stanley; he tried to fix it. He named Emin Pasha the expedition's official naturalist, going so far as to hand over his precious aneroid and thermometers—even giving the Emin lessons on using a sextant. A mistake, wasn't it? It only set the Emin off on other experiments, while Stanley waited on his approval for our departure . . . and waited some more. Then Stanley raged. Past the point of choler, Henry Morton Stanley delivered his ultimatum.

"We *will* march to Zanzibar on April tenth!"

True as ever to the master's word, the Relief of Emin Pasha Expedition moved out of Kivalli on April 10, 1889, leaving a burning camp behind. Now Stanley's prize was firmly in his grasp.

Meanwhile, I'd had time to catch my breath. Time to open my eyes again to the wonders of Africa. But did they fall on the flora and fauna? Or the scenic vistas?

Not bloody likely at this turn of my great Adventure.

My eyes went and fell on the fairer sex.

There I was, smitten.

And it was all on account of the Emin Pasha's daughter.

The Emin's daughter Ferida was six years old. That'd be our Hannah's age about now. But the two were like day and night. Hannah was snub-nosed, English fair, and quick as a whip. Ferida—well, considering as how her late mum was Abyssinian—Ferida was mocha smooth, with eyes like black diamonds, delicate features, and wavy ebony hair. She was a bright one, too, but in a lazy, fairy-tale princess sort of way. No surprise, right? Her precious papa doted on her, she rode in a hammock near the front of our three-mile caravan, and her servants'd face death sooner than let a fly light on her. Especially her nanny.

Ferida's nanny was another story, for a cert. She was wrapped up like one of those female presents back in Zanzibar. Curious how that makes the gentler sex so much more interesting than all the

bare-breasted women of the Congo put together. If my old friend
Seyyid had been around, he'd have poked me and whispered,
"Not to look, boss. Big trouble." But Seyyid wasn't around. And I
looked . . . and kept looking.

'Course all I could see were those eyes. Like a frightened
impala's, they were . . . a kind of liquid golden brown, beseeching,
drawing a fellow in. I knew the body beneath was a liquid golden
brown, too. What other kind of a body could be hidden beneath
layers of fresh cotton that wafted an exotic scent and spun dreams
straight out of the *Arabian Nights?* New words came to me. *Shiraz*
. . . *myrrh* . . .

"Watch where your mind wanders, brother!"

Tewfik caught me as I stumbled and near sprawled into the
razor-edged saw grass we were marching past. I steadied my legs
and gazed longingly toward the head of the caravan—toward the
Emin's donkey and Ferida's hammock, toward her nanny protectively walking alongside. . . .

"Allah preserve you," Tewfik prayed, as he steadied his load.
Then a hiss of warning. "This servant of little Ferida, Azzah,
is a married woman. Mohammed Effendi, the Emin's engineer, is a
jealous man."

"But she is surely younger than me! Too young to be married,
especially to that pompous, foul-tempered—"

"Nevertheless. We are too close to home to have you shot through
the back by such an Egyptian dog. And it would be through the back,
for the man is a base coward with all but his wife. Have a care."

"As you say."

I automatically resumed the chanted rhythm of the march,
blocking the temptress's call to consider Tewfik's other words. *Too
close to home.* Tewfik's home, not mine. I'd settle for Zanzibar,
though. Yet it was another 1,500-mile trek due east to the sea, and
the expedition only the third day into it. I shook my head. It
would be slow going with all the women and children suddenly
attached to us. In the end more than 500 of the Emin's people had

decided to join our caravan from Lake Albert. They were mostly Egyptian bureaucrats who'd chosen the station life for its excellent hazardous duty pay. In Equatoria the men could afford to amass vast harems and vaster households. Now the expedition was paying for their outrageous habits.

The vaster the household, the more things these people felt compelled to rescue with them. Fifty-one loads for the Emin Pasha himself. That could almost be justified. Most of his belongings were those specimens he'd collected for the British Museum. But fifteen loads for this lieutenant and twenty for that . . . added up, didn't they? And when some of them were iron bedsteads, and huge grinding stones, and ten-gallon beer pots—even *coffins*—and my Zanzibaris had to carry them. . . . Never forgetting the payload of ivory the Emin had gathered, the tusks averaging well over fifty pounds apiece. . . . *Bleeding Hell.* With the Egyptians taking advantage that way, Stanley'd had to round up more "volunteer" porters from the local tribes. Didn't endear us to 'em, did it? Now here we were with over 1,500 souls to march and feed—

"Halt!"

I quit worrying over those numbers as word filtered back.

"Early stop. Master sick!"

Blast. Stanley's stomach was acting up again. Zanzibar suddenly became 10,000 miles away. No point in even multiplying the distance to London. Henry Morton Stanley's digestion would cost us all dearly.

Four weeks is what it cost. Another lost month out of my life. Parke settled in for the duration with our stricken leader, but I couldn't spell him. Stanley went into a fit if I so much as approached his sickbed. He'd acted that way when ailing ever since his nasty bout of infection back at Fort Bodo. Should've been the other way 'round, by my lights. *Nevertheless,* as Tewfik would say. I set about looking for entertainment.

There was Ferida. It amused her to teach me baby Arabic. We

sat on the ground drawing extravagantly spiraled letters in the dust . . . with Azzah hovering above, correcting us. Hovering close enough to overwhelm me with her swaying robes, her fragrances. 'Nuff said. There had to be other diversions. When a gang of boys raced over our pretty pictures, destroying them, Ferida went into a sulk. Azzah hovered over *her*, and I began to use my mushy brain again.

"Achmed!" I yelled. "Hasan! Awab!"

The Egyptian lads barreled around and back again.

"You call, Bull Boy?"

"I do, indeed." I studied them. Strong, with energy to spare. Time it was put to better use. "How many of you young fellows are there in camp?"

"Oh, many, Bull Boy."

"Ten?" I held out two sets of fingers. Doubled them. "Twenty?" Finally I displayed them three times. "Thirty?"

"More!"

"Good! Then we'll have enough players for two teams of rugby. Thirteen each—" a quick flash of ten fingers plus three. "We can have proper matches. What do you think of that?"

Blank stares, then, "What is this rug-bee?"

Never crossed my mind that sheer ignorance would be an issue. Wasn't rugby flourishing across the empire? Last I'd heard it was giving cricket a run for its money as far off as New Zealand. "A game," I smiled. "A most excellent game with much running and kicking—"

"Ho. Running is good!" from Awab.

"*Kicking* surpasses it!" Hasan aimed a nasty blow at Awab.

"Here, now." I separated them. "We kick a *ball*. Mostly."

Achmed's brow furrowed. "What is this *ball*?"

Near gave up the entire enterprise then and there, but Ferida pulled out of her pout in the nick of time.

"Silly boys." She tossed all that lovely hair. Lucky for me she was six and not sixteen. "A ball is round and can be bounced."

"You've hit the nail square on the head, my girl." I turned to the rascals. "First we make a ball."

The bored camp got into the spirit of rugby, and soon we had a fine leather ball stitched up by the Emin's shoemaker. Not round, mind you, but closer to the regulation oval—though I'm not sure what England's finest would think of our hairy antelope skin hard-packed with browned-out grass. Next I lectured on the rules. Next we practiced a few standard moves and had some outstandingly enthusiastic scrimmages. Next we picked teams. Next Surgeon T. H. Parke came down with the fever.

"Doc," I griped, as I piled on blankets for the cold-dry phase. "You surely know how to pick your moments." I moved to a medicine chest to begin preparing an extra-strong quinine cocktail. From outside the stuffy tent came the shouts and cheers and groans of the camp's first rugby match kickoff. Life went on, didn't it? With or without Thomas Grenville Ormsby, manager of the Equatorial Greens.

"Sorry . . . Tom . . . missing . . . big match . . ." Parke's teeth chattered loud enough to drown out the uproar.

"Here, now. To survival!" I propped him up and tried to get the quinine past his mustache and down his throat. "Small matter, anyhow. Remember your Chinese proverb from way back? Just my turn to be responsible for you, is all. Got to be more important than rugby in the light of eternity."

When the fever hit Lieutenant Stairs next, the Emin Pasha himself spelled me in my duties. I'd near forgotten the man was a doctor on top of everything else. He was a good one, too, but a bear for organization. I would've thought a person who got wrapped up in science the way he did would be absentminded. Not a bit! The Emin set the medicines and instruments in order *precisely*, same as he did with his specimens and every object in his own tent, same as he'd organized his Equatoria stations. Then he'd squint near-sightedly at his patient and begin the healing.

So there I was, too overworked to worry about either rugby or matters of the heart. A good thing, too, since doctoring probably saved my skin.

Out of the sheer blue, Mohammed Effendi—husband to Azzah of the hidden delights—went berserk. The first sign was the spate of Arabic oaths roaring over the camp. The second was the Pasha's voice. "Peace, I charge you!"

"If you will not do me justice, I will kill myself, or my wife, or you!" Mohammed shouted.

I ran to the tent flap in time to see guards rushing up to subdue him.

He grappled with the guards like a madman, screaming, "Next I will kill Stanley!"

Could've added me to his list, too, if he'd caught me mooning over Azzah. The man was insanely jealous of near every male in camp. Why? One of 'em had to be behind his wife's not doing her duty by him! The Emin tried to reason with his engineer, to no avail. In the midst of the stalemate, Stanley hobbled out of his sickbed and into the glare of tropic sunshine for the first time in weeks.

"Bring me the man! Bring me the woman!" he bellowed.

Could probably hear him clear to Zanzibar. Our noble leader appeared to be convalescing. I glanced over at Parke. Hated to leave the doc in the middle of the hot-wet phase, but I figured he and his gallons of sweat would survive for a few minutes without my ministrations. It was me who couldn't survive without seeing what Stanley did next. I scarpered through the tent flap as Mohammed was shoved toward Stanley.

Once before the master, he insolently slapped off his guards. "I demand justice!"

"For what?" Stanley growled.

"Emin Pasha keeps my wife from her duties to me. Keeps her all night—"

Another batch of guards slung Azzah onto the ground before Stanley.

"He lies!" she cried, half-rising from the dust. "It is my own desire. To be with my Ferida, not"—she spat—"with that jackal."

So what does Stanley do? He bends down and rips the veil from her face!

Mercy. She's lovelier than in my wildest dreams.

"Speak, woman," Stanley barked. "What is your quarrel with your legal husband?"

"He beats me, Master! And steals my pay!" She crawled to Stanley's feet . . . touchingly lifted her arms in supplication. "It is I who needs justice. I will not return to him. *Ever.*"

Blistering Hell. To beat such a jewel. The bounder—

My fists were already tight and ready for work when Tewfik was suddenly at my side.

"Nevertheless, brother. Remember."

Wasn't easy, but I fought down my righteous wrath.

"*She* lies!" Mohammed raged. "But I take her back anyway, as is my due." The cad rushed for Azzah. She screeched. Stanley thrust out both arms and everyone froze.

"Enough. Here is my will. You, Mohammed, will take your wife. But you will swear never to lay a hand on her again. You will swear to allow her to keep the payment from her own labors."

Heartrending wails from Azzah. A satisfied smirk from Mohammed.

"I will swear to this." He laid hands on his wife.

"No . . . no . . . no . . . no . . ." Azzah struggled in his grip.

"Stay!" Once more Stanley intervened. "As she is unwilling, you may tie her up. You may keep her bound until her wifely ways improve. But"—he tried on a stern frown—"you will not otherwise touch or harm her. You will win her back to obedience through gentle ways."

Tie her up? Force her will? Without Tewfik's restraints, I would've attacked *Stanley*. Some Solomon *he* was. Instead I was compelled to watch good old Bula Matari do some smirking of his own as the Emin's guards re-appeared with ropes. Azzah fought them like a trapped beast.

Bloody, bleeding, blistering Hell. Blast, too.

But no amount of swearing in my head was going to change the situation. I sent Stanley a glare that would've crushed a witch doctor in mid-curse. Totally oblivious, he beamed on the happy couple, like he was about to raise his hands again—this time in a marital blessing.

"I have spoken."

My ardor cooled some over the next few days as Azzah's shrill howls echoed through the camp. Could be beauty was more than skin deep. Did I really want a woman who could swear better than me? Maybe she and Mohammed Effendi deserved each other. They seemed to be playing out some kind of game. . . . Then, when Stanley had almost recovered, we were back on the march with our leader guiding the long column from a hammock. My thoughts turned to the more normal worries of survival.

At the top of my list, as always, was food. It was at the top of Stanley's list, too. As we wound through the hilly grasslands of more tribes than I cared to keep track of, Stanley's philosophy on the subject remained the same: "Grain for bread and cattle for beef. The natives must yield these to people nobler than themselves."

When the natives didn't feel like yielding straight off, Stanley gave one of his little demonstrations with the Maxim automatic gun we'd been lugging. His first demonstration was a peaceful one . . . or so he said. Just after my nineteenth birthday it was, when we got a ceremonial visit from the fourteen-year-old prince royal of Ankori, whose father's domains we were currently trespassing.

Prince Uchunku was a smallish, timid sort of fellow, but he was buoyed up by quite an entourage, including witch doctors for a lavish blood-brotherhood ritual. When the ceremony with

Stanley was over and done and Uchunku grinning to beat the band in his newly gifted finery, Lieutenant Stairs made a big show of setting up our Maxim. It was fair impressive: the thick man-tall steel shield front and foremost; the gun—with the look of a baby cannon—poking its snout through the shield; the endless ribbon of cartridges ready to flow from its box; the gunner straddling the Maxim's supports, peering through its sights. Stairs milked the *ahs* from the prince's fascinated warriors, then aimed the gun at the nearest hill.

He let it rip.

Rat-a-tat-a-tat-a-tat-a-tat . . .

As round after round spewed out—faster than you could think, with eardrum-piercing power—Uchunku clapped a hand over his mouth and fair trembled. The Ankori warriors backed off right sharpish, too, pounding their spears into the dust and muttering behind their shields. The prince and his entire entourage cut and ran pretty fast after that. With the last of them melting over a distant rise, a beaming Stanley addressed his officers:

"There you see diplomacy in action, gentlemen. I believe we've now got free access to every plantation in the kingdom of Ankori. Word of mouth on the Maxim should see us through the next lot of kingdoms as well."

Diplomacy? Wasn't aught but more blackmail and pillage.

I turned on my heel and left as Stanley basked in his officers' "Well dones."

Don't even want to think about two months later, when we ran out of "word-of-mouth" kingdoms and set the Maxim up against neat ranks of Wasukuma spearmen.

In the meantime, the Emin's people began dropping like flies. They'd get cut, or stung, or burned by a cook fire, or pricked by a thorn—and refuse to tend to the wound. In that climate? Any idiot'd know that led to body-eating ulcers. Sunstroke, accidental drownings, and mysterious desertions in broad daylight all began assailing the caravan. This wasn't the jungle. There was almost enough to eat. Where was their stamina? It was as if they *wanted* to die. *Hell's bones.* The sheer waste of effort is what got to me.

Maybe it got to the Emin, too, because one afternoon while I was hurrying along our camp's setup under threatening skies, I watched Emin Pasha approach Stanley. As I sidled closer from sheer curiosity, I caught his question.

"My good sir. Might we not take the march easier?"

"Easier?" Stanley growled. "A mile and a half a day is surely easygoing."

"Then be easier still," the Emin pressed. "Aside from my natural concern for my people, there is yet much augmentation required for my bird collections—"

Stanley's face turned as menacing as the black clouds closing in. "By Heaven, Pasha! Do you wish us to stay here altogether? Then let us make our wills and resign ourselves to die!" And to the boom of thunder, Henry Morton Stanley stormed off.

The next day Stanley chivied the caravan into making a distance of two miles. The next it was three. And the next . . .

I figured we'd turned the corner and might actually make it to Zanzibar when we arrived at the palisaded mission station of Reverend Alexander Mackay of England's Church Mission Society. It was the first mission we'd found in over two years that hadn't been burned out or abandoned. There we discovered stockpiled goods and provisions that'd been sent inland from Zanzibar, awaiting the expedition's arrival since 1888.

Bloody Hell!

We stayed at the mission three weeks, during which time a letter caught up with Stanley from Bangala—clear on the far side of the Great Forest, near Stanley Falls. It contained the news that James Sligo Jameson was dead of the fever. Had been dead for an entire year. Was dead even as we rescued the remains of his and

Barttelot's rear column back in Banalya. Stanley's expression never changed as he read the letter to his assembled staff. Across the room, Mr. William Bonny gave me a knowing nod. That cannibal dinner flashed before me—then the warrior's head Jameson'd packed in salt and sent home. *Would it still be stuffed and mounted on a wall back in Ireland?*

After we'd fattened up at the mission, we were on the last lap of our epic journey—even though the expedition still faced almost three months of long marches. Gradually the comforting sounds of Swahili began surrounding us again. My Zanzibaris were so cheered that their marching chants began anew. With the chants, they near raced to the sea along the old Arab trading route that eased our last month's trek. We realized something odd had happened in our absence only when porters heading inland began hailing us with *"Guten Morgen!"* The mystery solved itself when Captain Freiherr von Gravenreuth and a garrison of German troops met us in mid-November.

The self-styled German "Lion of Africa" and Bula Matari, "the Smasher of Rocks," circled each other like dogs about to raise their legs over competing territory. The Emin Pasha had no such qualms. The man was sheer overjoyed to see a friendly face from home. While all this was unfolding, the stiff-necked German soldiers stood at painful attention in their too-tight, too-hot uniforms. They were good and red in the face, but it was fair obvious they hadn't *really* learned how to sweat yet. Poor sods. They would.

Next to me, Tewfik dumped his load and shook his head at the same sight. "While we were away, the sultan has become richer. Much richer."

"Sold out Zanzibar and beyond to the Germans, eh?"

"When a man marches in the jungle, in the bush, for three long years—"

"—A few things might've been happening in the greater world

beyond," I finished for him. "One of them being that Germany's decided to have a go at colonizing East Africa."

Tewfik rubbed his beard. "May Allah have mercy on us."

I held back a snort in deference to my friend. As far as I was concerned, the Germans were welcome to the entire continent. Africa would have its revenge on them sooner or later.

Right on the captain's tail were two American reporters hot to get the scoop on Stanley's expedition. After fawning all over the man, they hauled out stacks of articles written about us by the world's press—while we'd been away, mind you, and totally incommunicado. What an amazing lot of tommyrot! My favorite headline was, STANLEY DEAD BY SEVENTEEN ARROWS! Could picture that clear enough, couldn't I? Preferably by Pygmy arrows, lovingly poisoned . . .

The third day of December, we were close enough to the coast to hear the sound of the ceremonial evening cannon rolling across the waters from Zanzibar. On December 4, 1889, the Relief of Emin Pasha Expedition marched into Bagamayo, just a stone's throw from the island of Zanzibar itself. For the grand finale, Stanley and the Emin Pasha led the procession side-by-side on donkeys. Considering the fact that the two could hardly stand the sight of each other by this time . . . considering the further fact that they'd pretty much stopped talking to each other entire some months back . . . Well, it surprised me when Stanley turned to the Emin.

"There, Pasha. We are home at last."

Never seen such a look of sheer contempt pass over a man's face as passed over the Emin's when he finally acknowledged Henry Morton Stanley.

"Thank God!"

After Stanley and the Emin traded their donkeys for the fancy mounts presented by a delegation of German officers, Stanley made a production of turning over interim command of the expedition to Lieutenant Stairs. Then the rescuer and the rescued paraded through the town's main street en route to a fancy luncheon in their honor. I watched Stanley breathe in the cheering natives, the festive palm-branch decorations; watched his chest expand till he near popped his fancy buttons. Figured he'd be needing to size up his hat, too.

Behind, the survivors of the 1,500-mile trek from Lake Albert slowly straggled in—a mere 530 from the 1,500 with which we'd begun. Of these, near 250 were my Zanzibaris. *Bleeding mercy.* Never mind the hundreds of other porters we'd picked up and lost along the way. Out of the almost 620 Zanzibaris and Soudanese I'd personally inoculated on the *Madura* out from Zanzibar in 1887. . . *only these were left.* As for Stanley's white officers? Africa had taken its usual toll.

I turned toward the sparkling blue waters of the Indian Ocean.

Stop toting things up, Tom Ormsby. You're not a stock boy anymore.

What was I?

The elders of Bagamayo announced they'd be laying on an outdoors feast in honor of the surviving porters that night. For the leaders of the expedition, a gala banquet was scheduled for 7:30 PM in Bagamayo's German East Africa headquarters under the sponsorship of its commanding officer, Major Hermann von Wissmann. Word spread fast. Stanley's officers were invited. Mr. Bonny was invited. *Wonder of wonders.* Even I was invited!

"What do you think, Doc?"

I'd bathed and shaved and brushed my best Emin Pasha bush jacket. Now I paraded before him in the quarters laid on for us. He puffed on his cigar thoughtfully.

"Wouldn't mind being in your boots when you step off the dock in London, Tom. You'll be smothered by young ladies."

Guess I still knew how to blush, 'cause I could feel my

cheeks beginning to burn. "Here now . . ."

Parke laughed. "You'll do." He made a careless swipe at his own jacket. "I'm for some supper I haven't caught and burned with my own hands. Wouldn't say no to a glass of champagne, either."

"That makes two of us. For a cert!"

Oompahing for all it was worth, the band of the German gunboat *Schwalbe* was crammed against the banquet room's far wall. The food was served by sailors in immaculate whites, course after course. None of it contained insects. None of it was burned. The wine flowed. Most especially, the champagne flowed. Truth be told, despite my attempts at being cosmopolitan, I never had tasted champagne before. So what did I do? Went and inhaled the bubbles . . . and *sneezed.*

"*Gesundheit,*" Doc offered, trying his hardest to keep a straight face.

"Blistering . . ." I grabbed for my napkin. "I'll get the hang of it."

And I did. But once bitten, twice shy. I proceeded with a certain amount of caution. I finally relaxed enough to notice the other people around the tables—a bunch of Germans stiff in dress uniform, the Emin and his staff, our officers—and Stanley. Caught Stanley watering his champagne. Caught the Emin downing an entire bottle, without benefit of water. I went for another tingling sip and decided Stanley might have the right idea for once. After all, there were still the speeches to be gotten through.

So I sat back and listened to German marches and Viennese waltzes, wondering why they sounded so out of place. Wondering what the Africans outside in the night thought of the sounds floating through the second-floor banquet room's open French doors, over the veranda, and into the street below. Then I half-heartedly listened to the speeches. Noticed the Emin was having trouble swallowing the blarney, same as me. The deification of

Stanley went on for so long, his ex-excellency managed to polish off another few bottles of the bubbly. When the accolades finally ended, he adjusted his spectacles, swayed to his feet, and wandered between tables toward the veranda. Could use a breath of air myself, but first the strudel. . . . Maybe just another bite, and another—

"Bull Boy! Brother!"

"Tewfik!" I snapped out of my overfed lethargy fast. Only an emergency could make a Zanzibari brave this white stronghold. "What has happened?"

"Allah save us!" He bent over my shoulder and whispered, "After all our work, Emin Pasha has cast himself over the veranda into the street! Dedan stumbles on him and tears me from my feasting—"

Parke knocked back his chair. "Head out there fast, Tom. I'll tell Stanley and fetch my bag."

Had to shove my way through the shrill *lu-lu-lu*s of the ululating crowd outside the German headquarters building. There were my Zanzibaris, protectively circling the fallen Emin Pasha.

"He is dead." Bhoke dolefully poked at the body crumpled in the street's dust.

"Give me room, Bhoke, Dedan. All of you!" I waved off the bystanders. "Chap-chap!" Then I knelt over the Emin Pasha and began checking for signs of life. When Parke and Stanley arrived, I shared my diagnosis.

"Concussion, but no broken bones. We can probably thank the champagne for that. All those bottles the Emin drained? Relaxed his muscles enough for an easy landing after the fifteen-foot drop. His pulse is steady, but he's still unconscious—"

"Out of the way, Ormsby!" Stanley snapped. "Parke! See to the Emin! You boys"—he turned to my Zanzibaris—"stop gaping and bring a stretcher—"

Of a sudden, Major von Wissmann loomed over us all. Having

completed his duties as host, he took charge again.

"Your concern is appreciated, Mr. Stanley, but as commandant, I will now address this emergency." His decorations and ceremonial sword winked aggressively in the torchlight. "We have a fine German hospital in Bagamoyo."

The Relief of Emin Pasha Expedition officially retreated to the sound of Stanley's impotent growls. Scores of German soldiers appeared. The Emin Pasha, whipped onto a stretcher, disappeared. Stanley stomped off, and the Zanzibaris returned to their well-deserved feast. Doc took in the emptied street, the scattered campfires, and then turned to me.

"Your prognosis?"

"There were no skull fractures. The Emin'll have a nasty headache for a few days, but beyond that, nothing worse than a few aches and pains."

"Well done, Tom."

He pulled out one of his cigars and carefully lit it as we watched the Zanzibaris continue their interrupted celebration under the stars. The dancing. The music . . . its rhythms came so naturally to my ears now, routing the German band still droning above us. As it ought.

At last Parke spoke again. "If I had the authority, I'd hand you a medical diploma and license to practice tonight. . . . Have you thought about medicine, Tom? Seriously thought about it? I could write letters of recommendation to schools in England . . . "

The drums of Africa beat on in my head. Finally I shrugged. "It's all too much, Doc. First I need to get home. *Really* home."

"Amen to that." Parke sent more clouds of smoke into the night.

In the morning the German navy ferried the entire expedition across the Zanzibar Channel. I was assigned to the *Schwalbe*'s purser, and the two of us stood in tandem at the top of the gangplank, checking passengers off our respective lists. Almost hid behind my papers when Mohammed Effendi stalked up, his wife in suitable submission several steps behind. But Azzah never gave me a glance. Her liquid golden-brown eyes were red with rage, shooting daggers at her husband's back.

Flaming pity. Well out of that one, wasn't I?

Swallowing a chuckle, I got back to my list. Nearly everyone was checked off. Everyone, that is, except for the Emin Pasha— and Parke. Stanley paced the dock below, his blood pressure on the rise. Didn't like to be thwarted, did he? I almost felt sorry for him. So close to completing his coup, his prize had been stolen. The Germans weren't taking their hands off their catch, either. Von Wissmann'd even refused Stanley admission to visit the Emin in the hospital that morning. What did Bula Matari do about that? He made the Germans a present of Surgeon T. H. Parke to keep an eye on the Emin Pasha in his stead. Now poor Doc was stuck in the middle of the international mess.

The gangplank began its slow creak upward, and Stanley scrambled for it.

The second day in Zanzibar, Stanley ordered the final mustering of his expedition. The long-suffering porters stood at attention as of old, rifles to shoulders. I stood with another list in hand, ticking off names as my Zanzibaris relinquished their weapons in return for their well-earned pay. The rank and file received an extra forty rupees for their efforts, the surviving native captains sixty. I watched as Tewfik gravely accepted his bonus.

By Allah, the man deserved better than sixty rupees!

The Expedition's widows and orphans deserved better, too. Better than the ten thousand–rupee relief fund Stanley had convinced the sultan to subscribe to that very morning. How far could that go toward replacing husbands and fathers? I watched as the porters added to the mound of battered Remingtons. No more bugle calls before dawn. No more killing marches. No more campfires sending smoke above the jungle's canopy into the equatorial night. No more mournful Bhoke, or cheerful Dedan to buoy my spirits. No more wise Tewfik—

I shoved my list into a pocket and bolted after his disappearing robes.

"Tewfik! Brother! Wait!"

He paused and turned. "You call, Bull Boy?"

I halted, studying what three hard years had done to my friend. His arms were blackened sinewy cords . . . his chin beard had gone gray . . . his hair . . . . Enough. I flung my arms around him. "I will miss you so much!"

Tewfik gently pulled away. "The past life comes not back. Go with Allah, little brother."

I swiped at my eyes. "And you with God, Tewfik the Bold."

I spent my last few days in Zanzibar wandering through the bazaar and past the slave market that didn't officially exist. I studied with fresh eyes the tons of ivory awaiting shipment; saw every tusk steeped in Congo blood. I roved narrow alleys with crowded houses crumbling into each other—making way for the donkeys and camels laden with goods, ignoring the mangy dogs and beggar boys. The children no longer beseeched me for *baksheesh.* I'd made sure that this time I was one of them. At last. For I roamed in flowing robes and a turban, with a face dark enough and fierce enough for the Zanzibaris to make way for *me.*

I boarded the steamboat to Egypt in the same robes.

"Still fighting the call of the natives, Ormsby?" Stanley asked, as I sailed up the gangplank past him.

"Your officers are voyaging first class, sir," I answered. "My attire is perfectly suitable for a *second-class* passenger."

Stanley didn't rise to my bait. His mind was still full of the Emin Pasha. Stanley's prize had sent Parke packing to Zanzibar with word that he wouldn't be joining the expedition's party—

either back to Cairo or on to England. It seems the Emin had decided to stay in his beloved Africa. Only this time, he'd be working for the Germans instead of the British.

"Carry on, Ormsby."

I did carry on, near all the way to Alexandria. The night before our arrival, I was invited to join a private supper for all the surviving English in the expedition—meaning Mr. Bonny and me as well as Parke and Nelson and Jephson and Stairs. In honor of the occasion, I abandoned my robes for the old bush jacket.

"Well, gentlemen . . . "

Stanley paused to light an after-dinner cigar. His officers followed suit as a silent steward presented bottles of Madeira and Port. I leaned back from the table to open a porthole as the smoke swirled around us.

"—We haven't got the Pasha in the flesh, but by God, we did rescue him!"

"Hear, hear!"

Stanley raised his glass. "A toast. To the finest English officers an explorer could hope to have!"

"No!" Jephson squeaked. "To the finest leader of an expedition!"

More *Hear, hears.*

When they'd gotten all that out of their systems, Stanley announced that the Emin Relief Committee in London had seen fit to wire him good news: they'd voted a four hundred-pound bonus for his officers—as well as a two hundred-pound bonus for Bonny and me.

Bloody Hell. Second class to the bitter end.

Then the man sat back, beaming at this largesse, took another great puff of his cigar, and announced the rest of his plans.

"I'd like all you chaps to join me in Cairo while I deliver the Emin's people to the Egyptian government. Once that is accomplished, I intend to take a villa for a few months and write up my notes for publication. Expedition funds will put you all up at Shepheard's Hotel for the duration, from whence we can return to England as a group—the bold survivors of the Relief of Emin Pasha Expedition." Another puff. "What say you to that?"

What say I? *Bleeding misery.* Cool my heels for more lost months of my life while Stanley tarted up his exploits for his breathlessly waiting public? I glanced around the table, expecting protests. None came—not even from Surgeon T. H. Parke. His spaniel eyes just looked a little sadder. Enough. I scraped my chair back and rose. Stanley blinked.

"Eh, Ormsby?"

"Sir. With all due respect, I request permission to ship home from Alexandria tomorrow."

"What? And miss the glory?"

I widened my stance and squared my shoulders. "I believe I've already had about all the glory I can take. Sir."

Thwarted yet again, this time by a mere *dogsbody,* Henry Morton Stanley punched out his cigar. He bestowed his final glare upon me. "Then don't expect to be part of my memoirs."

"As you wish, sir." I turned to the other officers. "It's been an educational experience, gentlemen. Thank you."

Thomas Grenville Ormsby marched out of the Relief of Emin Pasha Expedition Club.

Above deck, I leaned on the railing, breathing in the humid air as the ship steamed through the final miles of the Suez Canal toward the Mediterranean Sea. My last night in Africa. Beyond lay England . . . London . . . my family. They wouldn't be welcoming back the same old "our Tom." Who would they be getting in his place? Engineer's mate? Donkey Tom? Bull Boy? Fito? The leader of Zanzibaris or the majordomo? The killer or the healer? . . . Maybe a bit of the lot.

I inhaled again, trying to suck in the very night. Could've saved myself the trouble. Africa was already in my veins—in every pore of my body. In my dreams and nightmares. Allah preserve me, there was naught to be done about it.

I threw back my head and laughed at the stars.

Was either that or cry, wasn't it?

AUTHOR'S NOTE

I went to Africa looking for a story. I found enough material about contemporary Africa to keep any writer busy for a lifetime . . . but I write historical fiction. So I admired the marvelous beasts that managed to survive the great white hunters and more current poachers and civil wars. I canoed the Zambezi River to Victoria Falls in the path of the fabled missionary and explorer Dr. David Livingstone. Then, on a long train journey through the heart of the continent, I began to read the travel memoirs of Henry Morton Stanley (1841–1904).

Stanley was the hard-driving British-American journalist and explorer who made his reputation by "finding" Livingstone in 1871—in what is currently Tanzania—as a publicity stunt for the *New York Herald*. During three expeditions to equatorial Africa and the Congo, Stanley had seen it all, done it all. His detailed reports became the catalyst for the European land drive for sub-Saharan Africa.

EMIN PASHA

Stanley's last expedition—the ill-fated Relief of Emin Pasha Expedition (1887-1889)—became the framework for my novel.

To tell the story well, I had to immerse myself in the Victorian era of empire building. I had to learn about the rampant colonialism that first began corrupting Africa, about the missionaries whose well-intentioned beliefs dispossessed the tribesmen of their identities, about the Arab slavers and ivory hunters already in place—and the tribes they hired to do their dirty work.

For the chronology, I relied heavily on Henry Morton Stanley's two-volume, 1,087-page recap of the Relief of Emin Pasha Expedition, *In Darkest Africa* (1891). I worked from a glorious illustrated first edition I'd picked up in the Welsh book town

of Hay-on-Wye some years back. To give the flavor of his character, I occasionally used a snippet of Stanley's words verbatim. I
also relied on John Bierman's *Dark Safari: The Life Behind the
Legend of Henry Morton Stanley* (1990). Bierman presents information
culled from expedition officers' diaries and private letters home,
which often contradicts Stanley's self-serving
report.

I also consulted scores of books on
Pygmies and missionaries and steamboats and malaria, and African
wildlife—not to mention Swahili gram-
mars and the *Qur'an*. I collected period
maps which convinced me to use period
spellings of place names, such as *Soudan*
for our current *Sudan*. And then there was
Joseph Conrad. His unforgettable Kurtz
in *Heart of Darkness* is probably an amalgam

HENRY MORTON
STANLEY

of Jameson and Barttelot, whose cannibalism and madness
shocked Victorian England to its very core on the release of their
papers to the public. I immersed myself in nine-
teenth-century Africa until, like Tom
Ormsby, it filled my dreams.

Tom is entirely my own invention.
He was inspired by the one European
member of the expedition that Stanley
refused to either name or write about—
his private servant. With the exception
of a few Zanzibaris, every other expedition member is an historical figure. The
surviving British officers died young:
Captain Nelson of dysentery in Kenya in 1892;
Lieutenant Stairs in the Congo the same year; Surgeon T. H.
(Thomas Heazle) Parke of a heart attack in Scotland in 1893;
Bonny in a poorhouse in 1899; Jephson of malingering fevers in

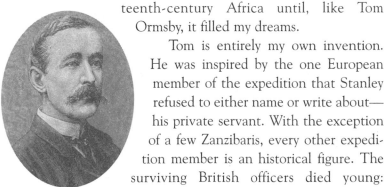

MR. JAMESON

1908. The Emin Pasha was murdered by
slavers in the Congo in 1892, but his
daughter Ferida was sent to Germany
and died there of pneumonia in 1923.
Henry Morton Stanley's expedition
days were over. He married Dorothy
Tennant, a fashionable English genre
painter, and renounced his American cit-
izenship in 1899 to accept a knighthood
from Queen Victoria. It was all he'd
ever wanted from the world to begin with:

MAJOR EDMUND
BARTTELOT

for the illegitimate Welsh orphan to be recognized in polite
society.

As for the people of the Congo themselves? In retrospect,
Henry Morton Stanley's attitudes and expedition tactics were fair-
ly benign. The plight of the native tribesmen only worsened as the
Congo Free State began building King Leopold II's railroad (1889)
from Matadi to Leopoldville along the route Stanley had blazed.

THE FIGHT WITH THE AVIVIBBA CANNIBALS

KILONGA LONGA'S STATION

With easier transportation available, the jungle was truly open to exploitation. Using the time-honored methods gleaned from centuries of the Arab slave trade, Leopold's *Force Publique* and its slaver and cannibal partners turned the Congo Free State into a vast slave-labor camp, slaughtering more than ten million Congolese—another hidden holocaust. When this "Rape of the Congo" caught international attention at last, the Belgian government was forced to annex Leopold's private country, and the Belgian Congo was born in 1908.

I've tried to tell the stories of all of these people truly and well. The events recounted happened. It's an amazing tale that caught me by the throat from the start. May it do the same for you.

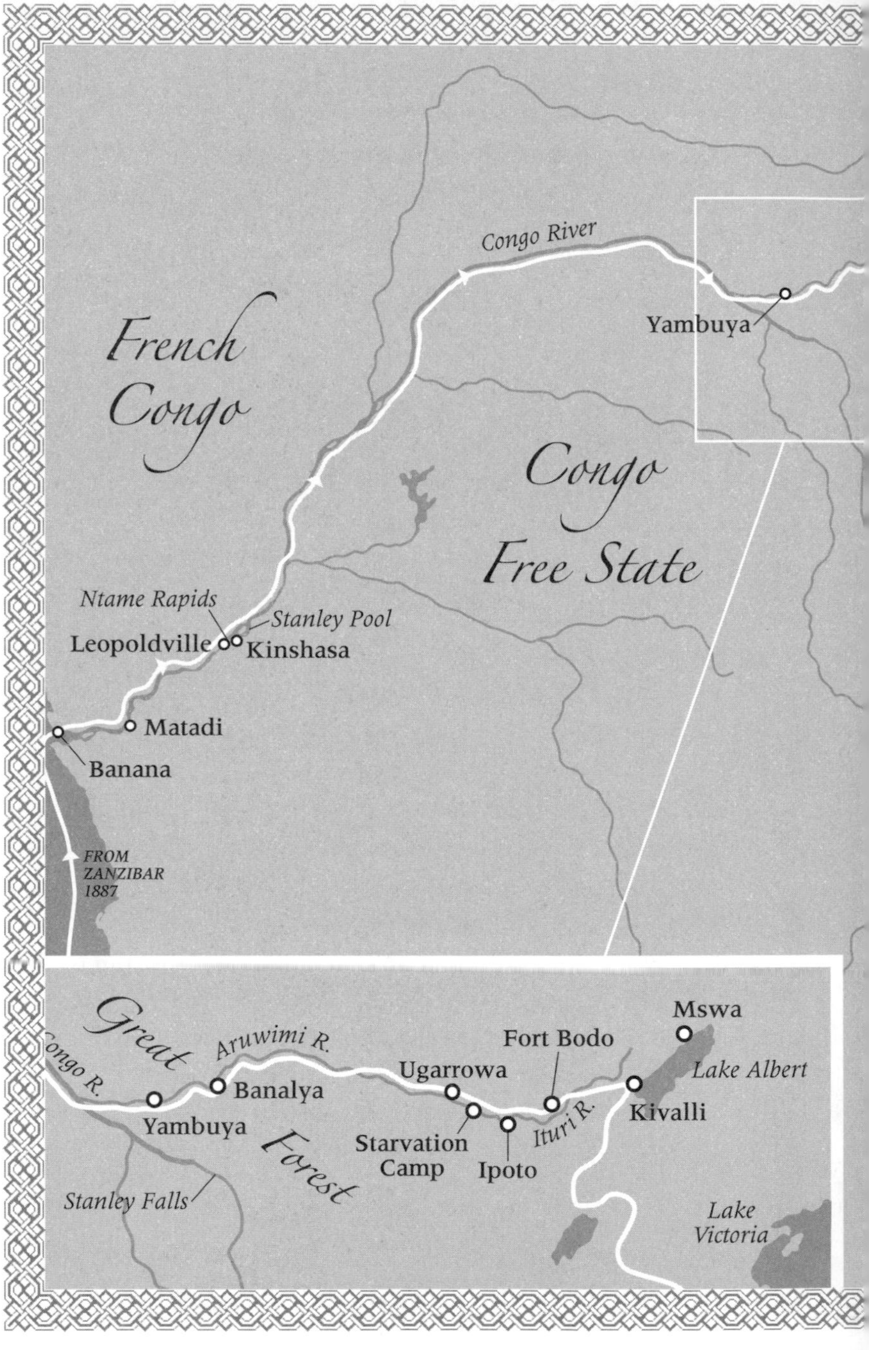

Congo River

French
Congo

Yambuya

Congo
Free State

Ntame Rapids
Stanley Pool
Leopoldville   Kinshasa

Matadi
Banana

FROM
ZANZIBAR
1887

Great

Aruwimi R.

Mswa

Fort Bodo

Congo R.

Banalya

Ugarrowa

Lake Albert

Yambuya

Ituri R.

Kivalli

Forest

Starvation
Camp   Ipoto

Stanley Falls

Lake
Victoria

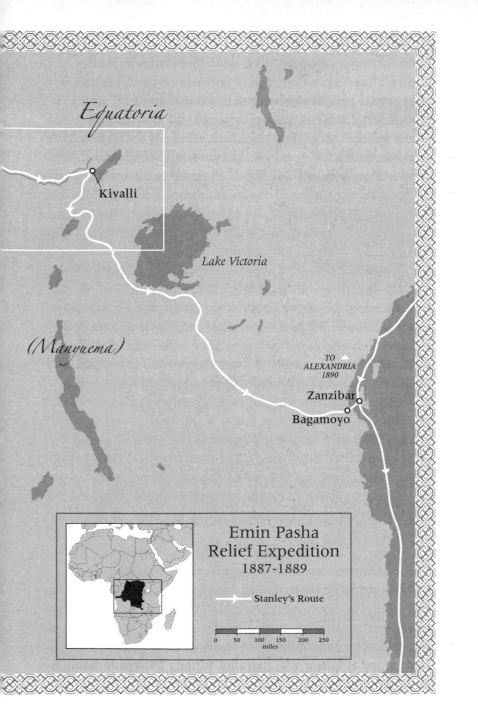

Equatoria

Kivalli

Lake Victoria

(Manyuema)

TO
ALEXANDRIA
1890

Zanzibar

Bagamoyo

Emin Pasha
Relief Expedition
1887-1889

Stanley's Route

| 0 | 50 | 100 | 150 | 200 | 250 |
miles

CHRONOLOGY OF EVENTS

1390–1665 ~ Kongo Kingdom
The kingdom developed a powerful centralized state and several provinces. It had its own currency of shells, *nzimbu*.

1784 ~ Kabinda
The Portuguese built a fort 30 miles north of the Congo's mouth, enabling them to establish slave stations along the river.

1807 ~ Slavery
Parliament abolished the British slave trade.

1838 ~ Slavery
Great Britain emancipated all states within its empire.

1841–1856 ~ David Livingstone
The 27-year-old David Livingstone (b. 1813, Blantyre, Scotland; d. 1873, Tanzania), a medical missionary, was sent by the London Missionary Society to South Africa to distribute the *Bible* translated into Sechuana. In 1845 he married a missionary's daughter and began his exploratory treks north. In 1849 he crossed the Kalahari Desert; in 1850 he explored the banks of the

Zambezi River above the Kalahari; 1852–56 he followed the Zambezi seeking a route into central Africa. He returned to Britain in December1856 and published *Missionary Travels and Researches in South Africa*, which made him a national hero.

1855 ~ Victoria Falls

In November, Livingstone was the first European to reach the falls of "Mosioatanya," or "the smoke that thunders." He was not impressed, as it had no useful function. He vastly underestimated both its length and width (actual: 1900 yards wide; 200-300 feet high). He renamed it "Victoria Falls" after the fact, as publicity to drum up British interest in colonizing the area.

1856–1866 ~ David Livingstone

Dr. Livingstone was a sensation on his lecture tours in Europe and America. Desperate to explore the African interior further, he resigned from the London Missionary Society. In 1857 he was sent back as British consul to Quelimane (Mozambique), and as commander of an expedition to explore central and eastern Africa. When his wife died in 1865, he returned to England. In 1866 the Royal

Geographical Society sponsored his expedition up the Congo River.

1869～Suez Canal

The canal opened at Port Said, Egypt, connecting the Mediterranean to the Red Sea and eliminating the months-long old route around Africa to the East. It was 100 miles long; its planning and construction (1859–69) were supervised by the French engineer Ferdinand de Lessups. Britain opposed its construction but in 1875 became its largest stockholder. The Convention of Constantinople in 1888 declared the canal neutral and guaranteed free passage to all in times of peace and war.

1871～Henry Morton Stanley: The First Expedition—the Search for Livingstone, 1871–1872

Stanley (b. Wales, 1841; d. England, 1904) emigrated to the United States before the Civil War and became a notable journalist. He covered, among other things, Indian treaty talks in the western U.S. and the opening of the Suez Canal. He was sent by James Gordon Bennett, owner of the *New York Herald*, to Africa as a publicity stunt to find Livingstone after the now world-famous missionary-explorer's expedition lost contact with the coast for four years. Livingstone was "found" in October 1871 at Ujiji in Tanzania. Stanley's greeting, "Dr. Livingstone, I presume?" received so much publicity that it became a stock music hall joke.

1872 ～ Henry Morton Stanley

How I Found Livingstone was published and became an instant best seller.

1873 ～ David Livingstone

Died in the jungle in June. His faithful native bearers buried his heart at the foot of a village tree, eviscerated and sun-dried his body, and carried it 800 miles to the British trade station at Zanzibar. He was buried at Westminster Abbey in April 1874.

1874 ～ Henry Morton Stanley: The Second Expedition—the Trans-Africa Expedition, 1874–1877

The expedition financed by the *Daily Telegraph* and the *New York Herald* descended the Congo to the Atlantic. Its principal results were that Stanley discovered and conferred his name upon Stanley Falls and Stanley

Pool—and his dispatches describing the vast natural resources hidden within the bush and jungle inspired King Leopold II of Belgium to dreams of empire.

1878~Henry Morton Stanley

Through the Dark Continent was published.

1879~Bula Matari

Stanley returned to the Congo to begin building his road from Matadi to Stanley Pool to circumvent the river's rapids. In the course of this Herculean effort, he was given the nickname *Bula Matari*, "Smasher of Rocks."

1884~Congo Free State

When the Berlin Conference of 1884 divided up Africa, King Leopold II of Belgium was made the "Protector of the Congo." He was responsible for building the largest forced-labor camp the world had ever seen, one that eventually killed 10 million Congolese. The United States was the first country to recognize the Congo Free State, due to the efforts of Senator John Tyler Morgan of Alabama, who wanted to send freed slaves there.

1885 ~ Fall of Khartoum

The British fortress on the Nile in Sudan was captured by the Mahdi and his forces on January 25 after a ten-month siege. General Charles George "Chinese" Gordon (1833–1885) was killed, along with his entire garrison. "Remember Khartoum" became a rallying cry for Great Britain.

1885 ~ The Mahdi

Muhammad Ahmed (1844–1885), grown fat, bloated, and besotted with his harem of wives, died in June—on the cusp of completing the destruction of Egyptian power on the Nile/Sudan. The self-proclaimed Prophet of Islam, he was the fanatical head of the "Mahdist" movement of soldier "dervishes" to overthrow Egyptian (British) rule, organized in protest over British attempts to prevent slave trading. He was succeeded by his right-hand man, Khalifa Abdullah, whose rule continued till September 1898, when his army was overthrown by Kitchener.

1887 ~ Henry Morton Stanley: The Third Expedition—the Relief of Emin Pasha Expedition, 1887–1889

Sailed from London in January 1887; arrived at the mouth of the Congo in March 1887; concluded in December 1889 in Zanzibar. Stanley's ill-fated expedition to "save" the governor of Equatoria trekked back and forth across the Congo's Ituri Forest (the dense rain-forest home of the Pygmies) three times, at the cost of hundreds of lives from fighting and sickness.

1890 ~ Henry Morton Stanley

In Darkest Africa was published, recounting the adventures of the Relief of Emin Pasha Expedition.

1908 ~ Belgian Congo

The country was formed after the Congo Free State was wrested from King Leopold II's personal possession due to an international outcry at his "governing" methods.

1965~Zaire

Mobutu Sese Seko seized power from the government of the Belgian Congo, renamed it, and continued the tradition of corrupt rule.

1997~Democratic Republic of the Congo

Seko was ousted and the country was renamed once more. Political and economic instability continued. Civil war was at its worst in the lawless northeastern Ituri Province (the Great Forest home of the *Mbuti*—Pygmy—tribes) where 60,000 people were killed between 1999 and 2006.